THE BLACKMAILERS

'THE DETECTIVE STORY CLUB is a clearing house for the best detective and mystery stories chosen for you by a select committee of experts. Only the most ingenious crime stories will be published under the THE DETECTIVE STORY CLUB imprint. A special distinguishing stamp appears on the wrapper and title page of every THE DETECTIVE STORY CLUB book—the Man with the Gun. Always look for the Man with the Gun when buying a Crime book.'

Wm. Collins Sons & Co. Ltd., 1929

Now the Man with the Gun is back in this series of COLLINS CRIME CLUB reprints, and with him the chance to experience the classic books that influenced the Golden Age of crime fiction.

THE DETECTIVE STORY CLUB

THE BLACKMAILERS

(DOSSIER No. 113)

A STORY OF CRIME BY
ÉMILE GABORIAU

TRANSLATED INTO ENGLISH
BY ERNEST TRISTAN

WITH AN INTRODUCTION BY
RICHARD DALBY

COLLINS
CRIME
CLUB

COLLINS CRIME CLUB

An imprint of HarperCollins*Publishers*

1 London Bridge Street

London SE1 9GF

www.harpercollins.co.uk

This edition 2016

1

First published in French as *Dossier No.113* by E. Dentu 1867

Translated as *The Blackmailers* by Ernest Tristan 1907

Published by The Detective Story Club Ltd

for Wm Collins Sons & Co. Ltd 1929

Introduction © Richard Dalby 2016

A catalogue record for this book is

available from the British Library

ISBN 978-0-00-813751-9

Printed and bound in Great Britain by

Clays Ltd, St Ives plc

MIX

Paper from
responsible sources

FSC
www.fsc.org

FSC™ C007454

FSC™ is a non-profit international organisation established to promote
the responsible management of the world's forests. Products carrying the
FSC label are independently certified to assure consumers that they come
from forests that are managed to meet the social, economic and
ecological needs of present and future generations,
and other controlled sources.

Find out more about HarperCollins and the environment at
www.harpercollins.co.uk/green

INTRODUCTION

ÉMILE Gaboriau's ingenious creation Monsieur Lecoq was
the first important literary detective to be featured in a series
of novels during the 1860s. Published midway between Edgar
Allan Poe's three celebrated stories featuring C. Auguste
Dupin (including 'The Murders in the Rue Morgue') in the
early 1840s and Arthur Conan Doyle's first Sherlock Holmes
novel in 1887, Monsieur Lecoq was also an exact contemporary of Sergeant Cuff in *The Moonstone* by Wilkie Collins
(1868), considered to be Britain's first classic detective novel.

Gaboriau moved ahead of his contemporaries by focusing
attention on the gathering and interpretation of evidence in
the detection of crime. Historically he is second only to Poe
in creating pure detective fiction, by writing the first novels
in which the nature of the crime, the role of the detective, the
misdirections, the reader participation and the solution are
all carried through successfully in the contemporary manner,
a great inspiration to all who followed in this genre.

Émile Gaboriau was born in the town of Saujon, France, on
9 November 1832, the son of a notary. He spent seven years
in the cavalry before settling in Paris, where he wrote poetic
mottoes for birthday cakes and songs for street singers.

He then became assistant, secretary and ghost-writer to
Paul Féval, author of widely-read criminal romances for
feuilletons (inserted as supplements in daily newspapers).
Gaboriau gathered much of his material in police courts
for Féval, and in 1858 broke away to begin work on his own
serialised novels.

After writing seven popular romances, Gaboriau produced
his first detective novel, *L'Affaire Lerouge*, which began its newspaper serialisation in September 1865, and was published in

book form the following year. In this story, Gévrol, chief of the detective police in the Paris Sûreté, is in charge, but the major detection is provided by Père Tabaret, an amateur consultant who explains his methods to the young Lecoq. Tabaret has studied the literature of crime for a long time and worked by ratiocination, or precise thinking, to solve a very deceptive crime, said to have been based on a contemporary murder.

Lecoq began in *L'Affaire Lerouge* as a minor detective with a shady past who had previously contemplated illegal methods of gaining wealth before joining the Sûreté. His career was inspired and closely based on the life and memoirs of the real-life detective Eugène François Vidocq (1775–1857), who also joined the Sûreté after a life of crime.

After his début, Lecoq had much more important leading roles in *Le Crime d'Orcival* (1867), *Le Dossier No.113* (1867), *Les Esclaves de Paris* (1868, initially in two volumes), and *Monsieur Lecoq* (1869, also in two volumes). These enthralling mysteries ensured that Lecoq gained countless admirers throughout Europe, including the statesmen Benjamin Disraeli and Otto von Bismarck. As Gaboriau's reputation grew, so were his novels translated and published in the UK, but none were more successful than the bestselling Lecoq quintet, issued by Routledge in the summer of 1887 in cheap paperback and yellow-back editions under the titles *The Widow Lerouge*, *The Mystery of Orcival*, *File No.113*, *The Slaves of Paris* and *Monsieur Lecoq*.

In addition to becoming a master of disguise, Lecoq developed valuable crime-fighting techniques, such as using plaster to make impressions of footprints and devising a test of when exactly a bed has been slept in. He was always a supreme master of excavating and analysing deeply-buried vital clues. Perhaps it was no coincidence that the first Sherlock Holmes novel, *A Study in Scarlet*, followed shortly after the Routledge paperbacks, at Christmas in the same year.

Émile Gaboriau died suddenly on 28 September 1873, supposedly of 'overwork', aged only 40, having written 21 novels in thirteen years (fourteen of them in his last seven years of life). He described his works as *romans judiciaires*, a crime-mystery form much imitated by writers in the century to come.

The third Monsieur Lecoq novel, *Le Dossier No. 113*, was first translated into English in 1875 and published by A. L. Burt in New York. The work was copyrighted to James R. Osgood & Co., but the identity of the translator was not given. Running to 145,000 words, the English translation was literal and rather cumbersome, although the book proved to be popular and was reissued by a number of publishers many times over the next four decades.

In 1907, a new translation by Ernest Tristan was published by Greening & Co. under the more evocative title *The Blackmailers*, a complete but more efficient interpretation of the book that halved its page count. It was this version that William Collins Sons & Co. of Glasgow later released in their rapidly expanding series of Pocket Classics. Also selected as the sixth book in Collins' new Detective Story Club imprint, it was published in September 1929 with typical fanfare:

'Émile Gaboriau is France's greatest detective writer. *The Blackmailers* is one of his most thrilling novels, and is full of exciting surprises. The story opens with a sensational bank robbery in Paris, suspicion falling immediately upon Prosper Bertomy, the young cashier whose extravagant living has been the subject of talk among his friends. Further investigation, however, reveals a network of blackmail and villainy which seems as if it would inevitably close round Prosper and the beautiful Madeleine who is deeply in love with him. Can he prove his innocence in the face of such damning evidence?'

The story was filmed in Hollywood in 1932 under the older title *File No. 113*, starring Lew Cody as the subtly renamed 'Le Coq'.

Although Gaboriau's fame and reputation were inevitably overshadowed by newer crime writers after his death, he was later championed by several discerning critics including the novelists Valentine Williams (in a 1923 landmark essay, 'Gaboriau: Father of the Detective Novel') and Arnold Bennett, who praised all the Lecoq novels in 1928, stating that they are 'brilliantly presented and, besides the detection and crime-solving, Gaboriau was able to provide a really good, sound and emotional novel'.

After 150 years, Gaboriau's novels will always deserve to be savoured, appreciated and rediscovered by connoisseurs of early detective fiction.

RICHARD DALBY
January 2016

CHAPTER I

THERE appeared in all the evening papers of Tuesday, February 28, 1865 the following paragraphs:

'An extensive robbery from a well-known banker of the city, M. André Fauvel, this morning caused great excitement in the neighbourhood of the Rue de Provence. The thieves with extraordinary skill and daring succeeded in entering his office, forcing a safe, which was believed to be burglar-proof, and carrying off the enormous sum of 350,000 francs in banknotes.

'The police, who were at once informed of the robbery, displayed their usual zeal, and their efforts have been crowned with success. One of the employees, "P.B.", has been arrested; it is to be hoped that his accomplices will soon be in the clutches of the law.'

During four whole days Paris talked of nothing but this robbery.

Then other serious events happened, an acrobat broke his leg at the circus, a young actress made her début at a little theatre, and the paragraph of February 28 was forgotten.

But this time the newspapers, perhaps on purpose, had been badly or inaccurately informed.

A sum of 350,000 francs had, it was true, been stolen from M. André Fauvel, but not in the way indicated. An employee, in fact, had been detained for a time, but no real charge was made against him. The robbery, though of unusual importance, remained unexplained if not inexplicable.

Here are the facts as related in detail in the report of the inquiry.

CHAPTER II

THE André Fauvel bank premises, No. 87 Rue de Provence, is an important building and with its large staff looks almost like a Government office.

The counting-house of the bank is on the ground floor, and the windows which look out into the street are fitted with bars, so thick and close together as to discourage all attempts at robbery.

A large glass door opens into an immense vestibule in which, from morning to night, three or four messengers are stationed.

To the right are the offices, into which the public are admitted, and a passage leading to the entrance to the strong room. The correspondence, ledger and accountant general's departments are on the left.

At the rear there is a little courtyard covered in with glass, into which seven or eight doors open. At ordinary times they are not used, but at certain times they are indispensable.

M. André Fauvel's private room is on the first floor in a fine suite of apartments.

This private room communicates directly with the counting-house by a little black staircase, very narrow and steep, which descends into the chief cashier's room.

This room, which is called the strong room, is protected from a sudden attack, and from a siege almost, for it is armour plated like a battleship.

Thick plates of sheet-iron protect the doors and the partitions, and a strong grating obstructs the chimney.

Inside these, let into the wall with enormous cramps, is the safe; one of those fantastic and formidable objects which make a poor devil, who can easily carry his fortune in his purse, dream.

The safe, a fine specimen by Becquet, is two metres high and one and a half broad. Made entirely of wrought-iron it is built with three walls, and inside is divided into isolated compartments in case of fire.

One tiny key opens this safe. But the opening with the key is quite an unimportant business. Five movable steel buttons, upon which are engraved all the letters of the alphabet, constitute the secret of its strength. Before putting the key in the lock it is necessary to be able to replace the letters in that order in which they were when the safe was locked.

There, as elsewhere, the safe was closed with a word which was changed from time to time.

This word was only known to the head of the firm and the cashier. Each of them had a key.

With such a property, though possessed of more diamonds than the Duke of Brunswick, a person ought to be able to sleep soundly.

There appears to be only one risk, that of forgetting the 'Open Sesame' of the iron door.

On the morning of February 28 the staff arrived as usual.

At half past nine when they were all attending to their duties, a very dark man of uncertain age and military bearing, in deep mourning, entered the office nearest the strong room, in which five or six of the staff were at work. He asked to see the chief cashier.

He was told that the cashier had not yet arrived and that the strong room did not open till ten, a large notice to this effect being displayed in the vestibule.

This reply seemed to disconcert and annoy the newcomer.

'I thought,' he said in a dry almost impertinent tone, 'that I should find someone here to see me, after arranging with M. Fauvel yesterday. I am Count Louis de Clameran, ironmaster at Oloron. I have come to withdraw 300,000 francs deposited here by my brother, whose heir I am. It is surprising that you have not received instructions.'

Neither the title of the noble ironmaster nor his business seemed to touch the staff.

'The cashier has not yet come,' they repeated, 'we can do nothing.'

'Then let me see M. Fauvel.' After a certain amount of hesitation, a young member of the staff named Cavaillon, who worked near the window, said:

'He always goes out about this time.'

'I shall go then,' said M. de Clameran.

He went out without saluting or raising his hat, as he had done when he came in.

'Our client is not very polite,' said Cavaillon, 'but he has no luck, for here is Prosper.'

The chief cashier, Prosper Bertomy, was a fine fellow of thirty, he was fair with blue eyes and dressed in the latest style.

He would have been very good-looking but for an exaggerated English manner, making him cold and formal at will, and an air of conceit, which spoiled his naturally laughing face.

'Ah, here you are,' said Cavaillon. 'Someone has been asking for you already!'

'Who was it? An ironmaster, was it not?'

'Precisely.'

'Ah, well, he will came back. Knowing I should be late this morning, I made preparations yesterday.' Prosper having opened the door of his room as he spoke went in and shut it after him.

'He is a cashier who does not worry,' one of the staff said. 'The chief has had twenty scenes with him for being late, and he takes as much notice as he does of the year forty.'

'He is quite right, too, for he gets all he wants out of the chief.'

'Besides, how does he look in the morning? Like a fellow who leads a terrible life and enjoys himself every night. Did you notice his ghastly look this morning?'

'He must have been playing again, like he did last month. I found out from Couturier that he lost 1,500 francs at a single sitting!'

'Does he neglect business?' asked Cavaillon. 'If you were in his place—'

He stopped short. The strong room door opened, and the cashier came in tottering.

'I have been robbed!' he cried.

Prosper's look, his raucous voice, his tremors, expressed such frightful anguish, that all the staff got up and rushed to him. He almost fell into their arms, he could not stand, he felt ill and had to sit down.

But his colleagues surrounded him, all asking questions at the same time and pressing him to explain.

'Robbed,' they said; 'where, how, by whom?'

Prosper gradually recovered.

'All I had in the safe,' he replied, 'has been taken.'

'Everything?'

'Yes, three packets of a hundred one thousand franc notes, and one of fifty. The four packets were wrapped round by a piece of paper and tied together.' With the rapidity of a flash of lightning the news of the robbery spread through the bank, and the room was quickly filled with a curious crowd.

'Has the safe been forced?' Cavaillon asked Prosper.

'No, it is intact.'

'Well, then?'

'It is none the less a fact that last evening I had 350,000 francs and this morning they are gone.' Everybody was silent; one old servant did not share the general consternation.

'Do not lose your head like this, M. Bertomy,' he said. 'Perhaps the chief has disposed of the money?'

The unfortunate cashier jumped at the idea.

'Yes,' he said, 'you are right; it must be the chief.'

Then, after reflection, he went on in a deeply discouraged tone:

'No, it is not possible. Never during the five years I have been cashier has M. Fauvel opened the safe without me! Two or three times he has needed funds and has waited for me, or sent for me rather, than touch it in my absence.'

'That does not matter,' objected Cavaillon.

'Before distressing ourselves, we must let him know.' But M. André Fauvel knew already. A clerk had gone up to his private room and told him what had taken place.

Just as Cavaillon suggested going to tell him he appeared.

M. André Fauvel was a man of about fifty, of medium height, and hair turning grey, who walked with a slight slouch. He had an air of benevolence, a frank open face and red lips. He was born near Aix, and in times of excitement he spoke with a slight provincial accent.

The news he had heard had disturbed him, for he was very pale.

'What is the matter?' he asked the employees, who respectfully drew back as he approached. The cashier got up and advanced to meet him.

'Sir,' he began, 'yesterday I sent for 350,000 francs from the bank to make the payment today of which you are aware.'

'Why yesterday?' the banker interrupted 'I have told you a hundred times to wait till the day.'

'I know, sir, I was wrong, but the mischief is done. The money has disappeared, without the safe being forced.'

'You must be mad or dreaming!' cried M. Fauvel.

Prosper answered almost without trouble or rather with the indifference of one in a hopeless position.

'I am not mad nor dreaming. I am telling you the truth.'

This calmness seemed to exasperate M. Fauvel. He seized Prosper by the arm and shook him, as he said:

'Speak! Speak! Who opened the safe?'

'I cannot say.'

'Only you and I knew the word; only you and I had the key.'

After these words, which were almost an accusation, Prosper gently freed his arm and continued:

'No one but I could have taken the money, or you.'

'You rascal!' the banker cried with a threatening gesture. Just then there was the noise of an argument outside. A client insisted upon coming in. It was M. de Clameran. He entered with his hat on and said:

'It is after ten, gentlemen.'

No one replied, but he espied the banker and went to him.

'I am delighted to see you, sir,' he said. 'I called once before this morning, but the cashier had not arrived and you were out.'

'You are mistaken, sir. I was in my private room.'

'This young man,' pointing to Cavaillon, 'told me so; but on my return just now I was refused admittance. Will you be good enough to tell me whether I can withdraw my money or not.'

M. Fauvel listened to him, trembling with rage the while, and then replied:

'I shall be glad of a little delay. I have just become aware of a theft of 350,000 francs.' M. de Clameran bowed ironically. 'Shall I have long to wait?' he asked.

'The time it will take to send to the bank,' M. Fauvel said, as he turned to his cashier and instructed him to write a note and send a messenger as quickly as possible to the bank.

Prosper made no movement.

'Don't you hear me?' the banker shouted.

The cashier shuddered, as if awakening out of a dream, and answered:

'That is useless, there is not a hundred thousand francs to your credit.'

At that time Paris was in a state of financial panic. Many old and honourable firms had gone to the wall, ruined by the wave of speculation which had swept over the country.

M. Fauvel noticed the impression produced on the iron-master and, turning to him, said:

'Have a little patience, sir, I have plenty of other securities. I shall be back in a minute.'

He went upstairs to his private room and returned in a few minutes with a letter and a packet of securities in his hand.

'Take this, he said to Couturier, one of the clerks, 'and go to Rothschild's with this gentleman. Give them the letter and they will hand you 300,000 francs, which you are to give to this gentleman.'

The ironmaster seemed anxious to excuse his impertinence, but the banker cut him short.

'All I can do,' he said, 'is to offer you my apologies. In business a man has neither friends nor acquaintances. You are quite within your rights. Follow my clerk and you will receive your money.'

Turning to the clerks who had gathered round, he ordered them to get on with their work, and then found himself face to face with Prosper, who had remained standing quite still.

'You must explain,' he said; 'go into your room.'

The cashier did so without a word, and was followed by his employer. The room showed no signs of the robbery having been committed by anyone not familiar with the place. Everything was in order, the safe was open, and upon the upper shelf was a little gold, which had been either forgotten or disdained by the thieves.

'Now we are alone, Prosper,' M. Fauvel, who had recovered his usual calm, began, 'have you nothing to tell me?'

The cashier trembled but replied:

'Nothing, sir; I have told you everything.'

'What, nothing? You persist in this absurd story which no one will believe! Trust me, it is your only chance. I am your employer, but I am your friend as well. I cannot forget that you have been with me for fifteen years and done good and loyal service.'

Prosper had never before heard his employer speak so gently and in such a fatherly way, and an expression of surprise came into his face.

'Have I not,' continued M. Fauvel, 'always been like a father to you? You were even a member of my family circle for a long time, till you wearied of that happy life.'

These souvenirs of the past made the unhappy cashier burst into tears, but the banker continued:

'A son can tell his father everything. Am I not aware of the temptations which assail a young man in Paris? Speak, Prosper, speak!'

'Ah, what would you have me say?'

'Tell the truth. Even an honest man can make a mistake, but he always redeems his fault. Say to me: "Yes, the sight of the gold was too much for me, I am young and passionate."'

'I,' Prosper murmured. 'I—!'

'Poor child,' the banker said sadly, 'do you think I am ignorant of the life you have been leading? Your fellow clerks are jealous of your salary of 12,000 francs a year. I have learned of every one of your follies by an anonymous letter. It is quite right, too, that I should know how the man lives who is entrusted with my life and honour.'

Prosper tried to make a gesture of protest.

'Yes, my honour,' M. Fauvel insisted; 'my credit might have today been compromised by this man. Do you know the cost of the money I am giving to M. de Clameran?'

The banker stopped for a moment as if expecting a confession, which did not come, and then continued:

'Come, Prosper, courage! I am going out, and by my return this evening I am sure you will be able to replace at least a large part of the money, and tomorrow we shall both have forgotten this false step.'

M. Fauvel got up and went to the door, but Prosper seized him by the arm.

'Your generosity is useless, sir,' he said in bitter tones; 'having taken nothing, I can return nothing. I have searched high and low, and the banknotes have been stolen.'

'By whom, poor fool, by whom?'

'I swear by all I hold sacred that it is not by me.'

A flush spread over the banker's face.

'Rascal,' he cried, 'what do you mean? You mean by me!'

Prosper bent his head and made no answer.

'In that case,' M. Fauvel, who was unable to contain himself, said, 'the law shall decide between us. I have done all I can to save you. A police officer is waiting in my private room, must I call him in?'

Prosper made a gesture of despair and said: 'Do so.'

The banker turned to one of the boys and said: 'Anselme, ask the superintendent of police to come down.'

CHAPTER III

IF there is one man in the world whom no event ought to surprise or move, that man is a superintendent of police in Paris.

The one sent for by M. Fauvel came in at once, followed by a little man dressed in black.

The banker hardly troubled to greet him, but began:

'I dare say you have heard what painful circumstances have compelled me to send for you?'

'I was told it was robbery.'

'Yes, an odious and inexplicable robbery, committed here from that safe you see open, of which only my cashier'—pointing to Prosper—'has the word and the key.'

'Excuse me, officer,' the cashier said in a low voice, 'my chief, too, has the word and the key.'

'To be sure, of course I have.'

The officer could see that it was a case in which each accused the other, and though one was the banker and the other the cashier, he observed them both very closely to try and draw a profitable conclusion from their manner.

The cashier was pale and drooping in his chair with his arms inert, while the banker was standing red and animated, expressing himself with extraordinary violence.

'The importance of the loss is enormous, 350,000 francs is a fortune. Such a loss might have serious consequences for the wealthiest of firms. Today, too, I had a large sum to pay away.'

There was no mistaking the tone in which the superintendent of police said: 'Oh, really?' The first suspicion had crossed his mind.

The banker noticed it and quickly continued: 'I met my obligations, though at a disagreeable sacrifice. I ought to add that if my orders had been carried out the money would not have been in the safe. I do not care to keep large sums here, and my cashier has orders to wait till the last moment before obtaining money from the Bank of France.'

'Do you hear?' the superintendent said to Prosper.

'Yes, sir,' the cashier replied, 'it is quite right.' This explanation dispelled the police officer's suspicion.

The officer continued: 'A robbery has been committed. By whom? Did the thief come from outside?'

After a little hesitation the banker said: 'I don't think so.'

'I am certain,' Prosper declared, 'he did not.'

Turning to the man who had accompanied him, the superintendent of police said:

'See if you can discover, M. Fanferlot, any clue which has escaped these gentlemen.'

M. Fanferlot, nicknamed the squirrel on account of his agility, had a turned up nose, thin lips and little round eyes. He had been employed for five years by the police and was ambitious, as he had not yet made himself famous. He made a careful examination and said:

'It appears to me very difficult for a stranger to get in here.'

He looked round.

'Is that door,' he asked, 'shut at night?'

'Always locked.'

'Who keeps the key?'

'The porter,' Prosper replied. 'I leave it with him every night when I go.'

'Is he here?' the superintendent asked.

'Yes,' the banker replied.

He opened the door and called:

'Anselme.'

This young fellow had been for ten years in M. Fauvel's service and was above suspicion, but he trembled like a leaf as he entered the room.

'Did you sleep last night in the next room?' the superintendent of police asked him.

'Yes, sir, as usual.'

'What time did you go to bed?'

'About half past ten; I spent the evening at a restaurant with the valet.'

'Did you hear any noise in the night?'

'No! And yet I am a very light sleeper, and the master's light footsteps, when he goes down to the strong room in the night, awaken me.'

'Does M. Fauvel often come down in the night?'

'No, sir, very rarely.'

'Did he come down last night?'

'No! I am quite sure he did not, for I hardly closed my eyes last night, as I had been drinking coffee.'

The superintendent dismissed him, and M. Fanferlot resumed his search.

He opened a door and said:

'Where does this staircase lead to?'

'To my private room,' M. Fauvel replied, 'the room into which you were shown on your arrival.'

'I should like to have a look round it,' M. Fanferlot declared.

'Nothing can be easier,' M. Fauvel replied. 'Come along, gentlemen, and you too, Prosper.'

M. Fauvel's private office was divided into two parts: a sumptuously furnished waiting room, and plainly furnished room for his own use. These two rooms had only three doors: one opened on to the staircase they had ascended, another opened into the banker's bedroom, and the third opened on to the vestibule of the grand staircase; by this door his clients entered.

After M. Fanferlot had glanced round the inner room, he went into the waiting room, followed by all but Prosper.

Prosper was in a state of utter bewilderment, but he was beginning to realize that the affair had resolved itself into a struggle between his employer and himself. At first he had not believed his master would carry out his threats, for though he realized how poor his chances of success were, on the other hand, in a case of the sort, the employer had much more at stake than his cashier.

At that moment the door of the banker's bedroom opened and a beautiful young girl entered. She was tall and slender and her morning wrapper showed off her beautiful figure. She was a brunette with large soft eyes and beautiful black hair. She was M. André Fauvel's niece, and her name was Madeleine.

Expecting to see her uncle alone, she uttered an exclamation of surprise at the sight of Prosper Bertomy.

Prosper, who was as surprised as she was, could do nothing but murmur her name. After they had stood for a few moments with bent heads in silence, Madeleine murmured:

'Is that you, Prosper?'

These few words seemed to break the charm and Prosper replied in a bitter tone:

'Yes, it is your old playfellow, Prosper, and he is accused of a cowardly and shameful theft; and before the day is over he will be in prison.

'Good God!' she cried with a gesture of affright. 'What do you mean?'

'Have not your aunt and cousins told you, mademoiselle?'

'No, I have hardly seen them this morning. Tell me what has happened?'

The cashier hesitated and sadly shook his head.

'Thank you, mademoiselle,' he said, 'for this proof of your interest; but allow me to spare you a sorrow by keeping silent.'

Madeleine interrupted him with an imperious gesture.

'I want to know,' she said.

'Alas, mademoiselle,' the cashier replied, 'you will learn soon enough my shame and misfortune.'

She tried to insist, to command, and then pleaded, but he had made up his mind.

'Your uncle is in the next room with the superintendent of police,' he resumed, 'and they will return in a minute. Please withdraw, so that they do not see you.'

As he gently pushed her through the door the others returned from their search.

But Fanferlot had kept observation on the cashier with the idea of finding out something from the expression of his face when he believed himself to be alone, and so had witnessed the interview. He at once formed a theory from it, which he decided to keep to himself for the present. He thought that they were lovers against the banker's wish, and that the latter had himself committed the robbery in order to accuse this undesirable suitor of it and so get rid of him.

The search of the upper part of the premises completed, the party descended to the cashier's office, where the superintendent remarked that their search had simply confirmed the opinions they had first formed.

The detective who was making a minute examination of the safe gave the most manifest signs of surprise, as if he had made a discovery of the utmost importance. The others at once gathered round and asked what he had discovered. After some hesitation he replied:

'I have found out that the safe has been quite recently opened or shut in a hurry, and with some violence.'

'How do you know that?' the superintendent asked.

The detective, as he handed him the magnifying-glass, pointed out a slight chafing which had marked the varnish for a distance of twelve or fifteen centimetres.

'Yes, I can see it,' the superintendent said, 'but what does it prove?'

'Nothing at all,' Fanferlot replied, though he did not think so.

This scratch seemed to him to confirm his theory, for the cashier could have taken millions without any need for haste. The banker, however, if he came downstairs quietly at night to rob his own safe, had a thousand reasons for haste and might easily have made the scratch with the key.

The detective, who had quite made up his mind to solve the mystery, was now more determined than ever to keep his theories to himself, as well as the interview he had witnessed.

'In conclusion,' he said to the superintendent, 'I declare that the robbery was not committed by an outsider. The safe has not been forced, nor has any attempt been made to force it. It was opened by someone who knew the word and had the key.'

This formal declaration convinced the superintendent, who at once said:

'I shall be glad of a minute's private talk with M. Fauvel.'

Prosper and the detective went into the next room, and the latter, in spite of his theories, was quite determined to keep his eye upon the cashier, who had taken a vacant chair.

The other clerks were burning to know the result of the inquiry and at last Cavaillon ventured to ask Prosper, who replied with a shrug of the shoulders:

'It is not decided.'

His fellow clerks were surprised to see that he had lost all trace of emotion and had recovered his usual attitude, one of icy hauteur, which kept people at a distance and had made him many enemies.

After a few minutes Prosper took a sheet of paper and wrote a few lines upon it.

The detective seemed to suddenly awaken out of a deep sleep, and the thought came to him that now he would find out something positive.

After finishing his short letter, Prosper folded it up as small as possible and threw it to Cavaillon, saying, as he did so, one word only:

'Gypsy!'

This was effected with such skill and sangfroid that even the detective was surprised.

Before taking action the superintendent, either out of deference or from the hope of obtaining more information from a private conversation, decided to warn the banker.

'There can be no doubt, sir,' he said as soon as they were alone, 'that this young man has robbed you. I should be neglecting my duty if I did not arrest him; afterwards the magistrate will either confirm his arrest or set him at liberty.'

This statement appeared to touch the banker, for he murmured:

'Poor Prosper!'

Seeing the superintendent's astonishment at this, he added:

'Till today I had the utmost faith in his probity and would have trusted him with my fortune. I almost went down upon my knees to get him to admit his fault and promised him pardon, but I could not touch him. I loved him and do so still, in spite of the humiliation I foresee!'

'What humiliation?' asked the superintendent.

'I shall be questioned.' M. Fauvel quickly resumed. 'I shall be obliged to lay bare to a judge my exact business position and operations.'

'Certainly, sir, you will be asked a few questions, but your well-known integrity—'

'But he was honest also. Who would have been suspected this morning if I had been unable to find 300,000 francs at once?'

To a man with a heart, the thought, the possibility even of suspicion, is a cruel suffering. The superintendent could see that the banker was suffering.

'Compose yourself, sir,' he said; 'in less than a week we shall have evidence enough to convict the criminal, whom we can now recall.'

Prosper received the news of his arrest with the utmost calm. His only remark was:

'I swear that I am innocent!'

M. Fauvel, who seemed much more disturbed than his cashier, made one last effort:

'There is still time,' he said, 'reflect—'

Prosper took no notice of him, but drew a key from his pocket and put it on the shelf, saying:

'There is the key of your safe; I hope you will recognize before it is too late that I have not stolen anything from you.

There are the books and papers my successor will need. I must tell you, also, that without reckoning the 350,000 francs you will find a deficit in my cash.'

At the word deficit his hearers became all the more certain of his guilt; even the detective became doubtful of his innocence. The explanation, however, which Prosper gave soon diminished the gravity and significance of this deficit.

'My cash is 3,500 francs short,' he said. 'I have drawn 2,000 francs of my salary in advance, and advanced 1,500 francs to several of my colleagues. Today is the last day of the month, and tomorrow we receive our salaries.'

'Were you authorized to do this?' asked the superintendent.

'No,' he replied, 'but in doing so I have merely followed the example of my predecessor, and I am sure M. Fauvel would not have refused me permission to oblige my colleagues.'

'Quite right,' was M. Fauvel's comment on the cashier's remarks.

This completed the superintendent's inquiry, and announcing that he was about to depart, he ordered the cashier to follow him.

Even at this fatal order, Prosper did not lose his studied indifference. He took his hat and umbrella and said:

'I am ready to accompany you, sir!'

The superintendent shut up his portfolio and saluted M. Fauvel, who watched them depart with tears in his eyes and murmured to himself:

'Would that he had stolen twice as much and I could esteem him and keep him as before.'

Fanferlot, the man with the open ears, overheard the expression. He had remained behind looking for an imaginary umbrella, with the intention of obtaining possession of the note Prosper had written, which was now in Cavaillon's pocket. He could easily have arrested the latter and taken it by force. But after reflection the detective decided that it would be better to watch Cavaillon, follow him and surprise him in the act of delivering it.

A few judicious inquiries as he was leaving informed the detective that there was only one entrance and exit to the premises of M. Fauvel, the main entrance in the Rue de Provence.

The detective on leaving the bank premises took up a position in a doorway opposite, which not only commanded a view of the entrance, but by standing on tiptoe he could see Cavaillon at his desk.

After a long wait, which he spent in considering the facts of the robbery, he saw Cavaillon get up and change his office coat. A minute afterwards he appeared at the door, and glanced to right and left before starting off in the direction of the Faubourg Montmartre.

'He is suspicious,' thought the detective, but it was simply a desire to take the shortest cut, so that he might be back as quickly as possible, which caused him to hesitate.

He walked so quickly that the detective had some difficulty in keeping pace with him, till he reached number 39, Rue Chaptal, where he entered.

Before he had gone more than a step or two along the corridor the detective tapped him on the shoulder. Cavaillon recognized the detective, turned pale, and looked round for a way of escape, but his progress was barred.

'What do you want?' he asked in a frightened voice.

With the civility for which he was famous, M. Fanferlot, nicknamed the squirrel, replied:

'Excuse the liberty I have taken, but I shall be glad if you will give me a little information.'

'But I don't know you.'

'You saw me this morning. Be good enough to take my arm and come into the street with me for a minute.'

There was no help for it, so Cavaillon took his arm and went out. The Rue Chaptal is a quiet street, well adapted for a talk.

'Is it not, sir, a fact,' began the detective, 'that M. Prosper Bertomy threw you a note this morning?'

'You are mistaken,' he replied, blushing.

'I should be sorry to say you were not telling the truth, unless I were sure.'

'I assure you Prosper gave me nothing.'

'Pardon me, sir, but do not deny it,' Fanferlot said, 'or you will force me to prove that four of your fellow-clerks saw him throw you a note.'

Seeing that denial was useless, the young man changed his method.

'Yes, that is quite right; I received a note from Prosper, but it was private, and after reading it I tore it up and threw the pieces in the fire.'

It was very likely that this was true, but Fanferlot decided to take his chance.

'Allow me, sir, to remark that is not correct; the note was to be delivered to Gypsy.'

Cavaillon made a despairing gesture which told the detective that he was right, and began:

'I swear to you, sir—'

'Do not swear at all, sir,' Fanferlot interrupted; 'all the oaths in the world are useless. You have the note in your pocket and entered that house to deliver it.'

'No, sir; no.' The detective took no notice of the denial and went on:

'You will be good enough to let me read the note.'

'Never,' Cavaillon replied.

Thinking this was a favourable opportunity, the young man tried to free his arm, but the detective was as strong as he was polite.

'Take care not to injure yourself, young man,' the detective said, 'and give me the note.'

'I have not got it.'

'Come; you will force me to adopt unpleasant measures. Do you know what will happen? I shall call two policemen and have you arrested and searched.'

It seemed to Cavaillon, devoted to Prosper though he was, that the struggle was now useless, and he did not even have the opportunity to destroy the note. To deliver up the note under these circumstances was not betraying a trust.

'You are the stronger,' he said; 'I obey.' He took the note from his case, cursing his own powerlessness as he did so, and handed it to the detective, whose hands trembled with pleasure as he opened it and read:

'DEAR NINA,

'If you love me, obey me quickly without a moment's hesitation. When you receive this, take everything belonging to you—*everything*, and go and live in a furnished house at the other end of Paris. Do not show yourself; disappear as much as possible. On your obedience my life perhaps depends. I am accused of a large robbery and I am going to be arrested. There should be 500 francs in the drawer; take it. Give your address to Cavaillon and he will explain to you what I cannot tell you.

'PROSPER.'

Had Cavaillon been less occupied with his own thoughts, he would have noticed a look of disappointment on the detective's face. Fanferlot had hoped that this note was of importance, but it seemed to be merely a love-letter. The word 'everything' was, it was true, underlined, but that might mean anything.

'Is Madame Nina Gypsy,' the detective asked Cavaillon, 'a friend of M. Prosper Bertomy?'

'She is his mistress.'

'She lives at No. 39, does she not?'

'You know very well she does, for you saw me go in.'

'Does she occupy rooms in her own name?'

'No, she lives with Prosper.'

'On what floor?'

'The first.'

M. Fanferlot carefully refolded the note and put it in his pocket.

'I am much obliged,' he said, 'for your information, and in return I will deliver the letter for you.'

Cavaillon offered some resistance to this, but M. Fanferlot cut him short with these words:

'I will give you some good advice. If I were in your place, I would go back to the office and have no more to do with this affair.

'But he is my friend and protector.'

'All the more reason you should keep quiet. How can you help him? You are more likely to do him harm.'

'But, sir, I am sure Prosper is innocent.'

That was, too, Fanferlot's opinion; but he did not consider it wise to tell the young man this, so he said:

'It is quite possible, and I hope it is so for M. Bertomy's sake, and also for your sake, for if he is found guilty, you may be suspected too. So, go back to your work.'

The poor fellow obeyed with a heavy heart, wondering how he could help Prosper and warn Madame Gypsy.

As soon as he had disappeared, Fanferlot went over to the house and rang the first-floor bell. It was answered by a page to whom he showed the note when he asked to see the lady. He was shown into a beautifully-furnished drawing-room, and Madame Nina Gypsy came in at once.

She was a frail, delicate little woman, a brunette or rather golden, like a Havanna quadroon, with the feet and hands of a child. She had long silky lashes and large black eyes, and her lips, which were a little thick, displayed when she smiled the most beautiful white teeth.

She was not yet dressed, but appeared very charming in a velvet wrapper, and the detective was at first quite dazzled. She seemed surprised to see this shabby looking person in her drawing-room and at once assumed her most disdainful manner.

'What do you want?' she asked.

'I have a note to give you,' said the detective in his most humble voice, 'from M. Bertomy.'

'From Prosper! Do you know him?'

'I have the honour, and if I dare use the expression, I am one of his friends, one of the few who now have the courage to admit their friendship.'

The detective looked so serious that Madame Gypsy was impressed.

'I am not clever at riddles,' she said dryly; 'what do you mean to insinuate?'

He took the letter from his pocket and handed it to the lady, saying as he did so:

'Read this.'

Adjusting an eye-glass to her charming eyes she read the note at one glance. First she turned pale, then she became flushed and trembled as if she were about to faint. But in an instant she pulled herself together, and seizing the detective's wrists in a grip which made him cry out:

'Explain,' she said; 'what does it mean? You know what this letter says?'

Brave as he was, Fanferlot was almost afraid of Madame Nina's anger.

'Prosper is accused of taking 350,000 francs from his safe,' he murmured.

'Prosper a thief!' she said; 'how foolish. Why should he be a thief? He is well off, isn't he?'

'No; people say he is not rich, but has to live upon his salary.'

This reply seemed to confuse Madame Gypsy's ideas.

'But,' she insisted, 'he always has plenty of money—'

She dared not finish her sentence, for it suddenly occurred to her that if he were a thief it would be for her. But after a few seconds' reflection her doubts disappeared.

'No,' she cried, 'Prosper has never stolen a half-penny for me. A cashier might steal for the woman he loved, but Prosper does not love me and has never done so.'

'Beautiful lady,' protested the polite Fanferlot, 'you don't mean that.'

'I do,' she replied with tears in her eyes, 'and it is true. He humours my fancies, but that proves nothing. I am nothing in his life—hardly an accident.'

'But why—?'

'Yes,' Madame Gypsy interrupted, 'why? You will be clever if you can tell me. I have tried to find out for a year. It is impossible to read the heart of a man who is so far master of himself that what is passing in his heart never mounts to his eyes. People think he is weak, but they are mistaken. This man with blonde hair is like a bar of steel painted like a reed.'

Carried away by the violence of her sentiments, Madame Nina was laying bare her heart to this man whom she believed was a friend of Prosper's, while the detective was complimenting himself upon his skill in obtaining all this valuable information.

'It has been said,' he suggested, 'that M. Bertomy is a great gambler.'

Madame Gypsy shrugged her shoulders.

'Yes, that is true,' she replied. 'I have seen him win or lose considerable sums without a tremor, but he is not a gambler. He gambles in the same way that he sups and gets drunk— without passion and pleasure, but with a profound indifference which sometimes seems to me almost like despair. Nothing will ever remove the idea from my mind that he has a terrible secret in his life.'

'Has he never spoken to you of the past?'

'Did you not hear me tell you that he did not love me?'

Madame Nina began to weep, but after a few minutes her generous impulses told her that it was no time for despair.

'But I love him,' she cried, 'and I must save him. I will speak to his employer and the judges, and before the day is over he will be free, or I shall be prisoner with him.'

This plan, though dictated by the most noble motives, did not meet with the detective's approval, for he did not propose that the lady should appear till what he considered to be the proper moment. He therefore set to work to calm her and show the weakness of her plan.

'What will you gain, dear lady?' he said; 'you have no chance of success and may be seriously compromised and treated as an accomplice.'

'What does the danger matter?' she cried. 'I don't think there is any; but if it exists, so much the better: it will give a little merit to a natural effort. I am sure Prosper is innocent, but if by any possible chance he is guilty, I wish to share his punishment.'

Madame Gypsy put on her hat and called upon Fanferlot to accompany her. But he had still several strings to his bow. As personal considerations had no weight with this lady he decided to introduce as an argument Prosper's own interests.

'I am ready, lady,' he replied; 'let us go. Only, while there is still time, let me tell you we shall probably do M. Bertomy more harm than good by taking a step he did not anticipate when he wrote to you.'

'Some people,' the young woman answered, 'have to be rescued against their will. I know Prosper; he is the man to allow himself to be killed without a struggle—'

'Excuse me, dear madame,' the detective interrupted, 'M. Bertomy does not seem to me that kind of man. I believe he has already fixed upon his line of defence, and perhaps by showing yourself at the wrong time you will destroy his most certain way of justifying himself.'

Madame Gypsy delayed her answer to consider Fanferlot's objections.

'But I cannot,' she said, 'remain inactive without trying to contribute to his safety.'

The detective, feeling that he had gained his point, said:

'You have a simple way to serve the man you love, and that is to obey him; that is your sacred duty.'

She hesitated, so he picked up Prosper's letter from the table and continued:

'M. Bertomy when he is just about to be arrested writes to you and tells you to go away and hide, if you love him, and yet you hesitate. He has reasons for saying so you may be sure.'

M. Fanferlot had himself guessed the reason as soon as he entered the room, but he was keeping that in reserve.

Madame Gypsy was intelligent enough also to divine the reason.

'Reasons!' she began; 'perhaps Prosper wished our liaison to remain a secret! No. I understand now. My presence here would be a serious charge against him. They would ask how he could give me all these things, and where he obtained the money to do so.'

The detective bowed his head in assent.

'Then I must fly at once! Perhaps the police know already and will be here directly.'

'Oh,' Fanferlot said, 'there is plenty of time.'

She rushed out of the room, calling her servants, and told them to put everything into her boxes as quickly as possible. She herself set the example. Suddenly an idea struck her and she went back to Fanferlot.

'Everything is ready,' she said, 'but where am I to go?'

'M. Bertomy said furnished rooms at the other end of Paris.'

'But I do not know any.'

The detective seemed to reflect for a moment, and then, making every effort to conceal his joy at the idea, said:

'I know a hotel where with an introduction from me you would be treated like a little queen, though it is not so luxurious as here.'

'Where is it?'

'On the other side of the water, the *Hôtel du Grand-Archange*, Quai Saint-Michel, kept by Madame Alexandré.

Nina never took long to make up her mind.

'Here is the ink,' she said, 'write the introduction.'

He had finished in a moment.

'With these three lines, lady,' he said, 'you will be well looked after.'

'Very well! Now I must let Cavaillon know my address. He should have brought the letter—'

'He could not come,' the detective interrupted, 'but I am going to see him and will let him know your address.

Madame Gypsy was about to send for a carriage, when Fanferlot volunteered to procure one for her. He stopped one as it was passing and instructed the driver to wait for a little dark lady, and if she ordered him to drive to the Quai Saint-Michel he was to crack his whip; but if she gave him any other address he was to get down from his box as if to put one of the traces right.

The detective crossed the road, entered a wine-shop opposite, and a minute afterwards the loud cracking of a whip disturbed the quiet street. Madame Nina had gone to the *Grand-Archange*.

The detective rubbed his hands with glee.

CHAPTER IV

WHILE Madame Nina Gypsy was on her way to the *Grand-Archange*, Prosper Bertomy was at the police station.

He was kept waiting there for two hours, during which time he talked to the two policemen in whose charge he was. His expression never varied, his face was like marble. At midday he sent for lunch from a neighbouring restaurant, ate it with a good appetite, and drank almost a whole bottle of wine.

During this time ten other officers at least came to look at him, and they all expressed their views in similar terms. They said:

'He is a stubborn fellow.'

When he was told that a carriage was waiting, he got up quickly, asked permission to light a cigar, and went downstairs. At the door he bought a buttonhole from a flower girl who wished him good luck.

He thanked her and got into the carriage which drove along the Rue Montmartre.

It was a lovely day, and he remarked to his guardians:

'It is very strange, but I never felt so much like a walk before.'

One of them replied, 'I can quite believe that.'

At the clerk's office, while the entries were being made in the gaol book, Prosper answered the questions with disdainful hauteur. But when he was told to empty his pockets, a gleam of indignation shot from his eyes. He would perhaps have been subjected to further indignities but for the intervention of an oldish man of distinguished appearance, wearing a white necktie and gold-rimmed spectacles, who was warming himself at a stove and appeared quite at home. This was a noted member of the detective force, M. Lecoq, whose eyes had been intently fixed upon the cashier, and who had displayed considerable surprise at his entrance.

After the usual formalities had been completed the cashier was removed to a cell, where as soon as he was alone he burst into tears. His pent-up anger got beyond control; he shouted, cursed, blasphemed and beat the walls with his fists.

Prosper Bertomy was not what he appeared to be, he had ardent passions and a fiery temperament. One day at the age of twenty-four he was seized with ambition and a desire to be like the rich men he saw around him. He studied the careers of these financiers and discovered that at first they were worse off than he was, but that by energy, intelligence and audacity they had succeeded.

He swore to imitate them, and from that time he silenced his instincts and reformed not his character, but its outward appearance.

His efforts had not been wasted. Those who knew him said he was a coming man. But here he was in prison, and even if he were not guilty he would be marked as a suspected man.

The following morning—he had just gone to sleep after a sleepless night—he was awakened for his examination.

As the warder conducted him, he said:

'You are fortunate; you have to deal with a good brave man.'

He was right. M. Patrigent possessed in a remarkable degree all the qualities necessary for a magistrate. He was keen, firm, unbiased, neither too lenient nor too severe, but a man of inexhaustible patience. This was the man before whom Prosper had to appear.

After walking a considerable distance the warder and his charge entered a long narrow gallery in which were several numbered doors, each of which admitted to the presence of a magistrate.

'Here,' the warder said, 'your fate will be decided.'

The cashier and his guardian sat down upon an oak bench in the gallery which had already numerous occupants, to wait their turn. Groups of witnesses and gendarmes stood talking in low tones in the gallery, and at short intervals a door opened and an usher called out a name or number.

At last the usher called 'Prosper Bertomy!'

The cashier on leaving the dark gallery suddenly found himself almost blinded by the light from the window of the courtroom.

The courtroom had nothing striking about it. It contained a large desk at which the magistrate sat with his face in shadow and with the light shining full in the faces of the accused and the witness. On his right was his clerk.

Prosper's attention was, however, fixed upon the magistrate's face, and he soon realized that the warder was right, for he had an attractive and reassuring face.

'Take a chair,' he said to Prosper, who was favourably impressed by this attention and took it as a good omen.

M. Patrigent made a sign to the clerk and said:

'We are ready to begin, Sigault.'

Turning to Prosper, he asked:

'What is your name?'

'Auguste Prosper Bertomy, sir.'

'How old are you?'

'I shall be thirty-five on the fifth of May.'

'What is your occupation?'

'I am, or rather I was the cashier at the André Fauvel Bank.'

The magistrate stopped to consult his papers and then asked:

'Where do you live?'

'At 39, Rue Chaptal for the last four years. Before that I lived at No. 7, Boulevard des Bategnolles.'

'Where were you born?'

'At Beaucaire, in the Department du Gard.'

'Are your parents alive?'

'I lost my mother two years ago, but my father is still alive.'

'Does he live in Paris?'

'No, sir, he lives at Beaucaire with my sister, who married an engineer of the Midi Canal.'

Prosper replied to the last question in a troubled voice. There are times in a man's life when the remembrance of his relations consoles him, but there are also times when he wishes to be alone in the world.

M. Patrigent noted his emotion and continued:

'What is your father's profession?'

'He was, sir, employed on the Midi Canal; now he has retired.'

'You are accused of stealing 350,000 francs from your employer. What have you to say?'

'I am innocent, sir; I swear I am innocent!'

'I hope so,' M. Patrigent said, 'and you can count on my assistance in proving your innocence. Have you any facts to mention in your defence?'

'Sir, what can I say? I can only invoke my whole life.'

The magistrate interrupted. 'Let us be precise; the robbery was committed in such a way that suspicion can only rest upon M. Fauvel and you. Can you throw suspicion on anyone else?'

'No, sir.'

'You say you are innocent, so M. Fauvel must be the criminal.'

Prosper made no answer.

'Have you,' M. Patrigent insisted, 'any reason to think your employer robbed himself? Tell me it, however trifling it may be.'

As he made no reply the magistrate said:

'I see you still need time for reflection. Listen to the reading of your evidence, and after you have signed it you will return to prison.'

The cashier was overwhelmed by these words. He signed the statement without hearing a word of the reading and staggered so on leaving the courtroom that the warder told him to lean upon him and take courage.

His examination was a formality carried out in obedience to the law, which ordered that a prisoner was to be examined within twenty-four hours of his arrest.

Had Prosper remained an hour longer in the gallery, he would have heard the same usher call out 'number three'.

The witness who was number three was sitting on the bench in the person of M. Fauvel. He was a changed man. His ordinary benevolence had disappeared and he was full of resentment against his cashier.

He had hardly answered the usual questions before he launched out into such recriminations and invectives against Prosper that the magistrate had to silence him.

'Let us take things in their proper order,' he said to M. Fauvel, 'and please confine yourself to answering my questions.

'Did you doubt your cashier's honesty?'

'Certainly not; and yet a thousand reasons might have led me to do so.'

'What reasons were they?'

'M. Bertomy, my cashier, gambled and sometimes lost large sums. On one occasion, with one of my clients, he was mixed up in a scandalous gaming affair, which began with a woman and ended with the police.'

'You must admit, sir,' the magistrate said, 'you were imprudent, if not culpable, to entrust your cash to such a man.'

'But, sir,' M. Fauvel replied, 'he was not always like it. Till a year ago he was a model. He resided in my house and I believed him to be in love with my niece Madeleine.'

M. Patrigent had a way of knitting his brows when he thought he had made a discovery.

'Perhaps that was the reason of his departure?' the magistrate asked.

'Why,' the banker replied with a surprised look, 'I would have willingly given him my niece's hand, and she is a pretty girl with money.'

'Then you can see no motive in your cashier's conduct?'

'Absolutely none,' the banker replied, after a little thought. 'I always thought he was led astray by a young man he knew at that time, M. Raoul de Lagors.'

'Who is he?'

'A relative of my wife's, a charming fellow, but rich enough to pay for his amusement.'

The magistrate did not seem to be listening, he was adding Lagors to his long list of names.

'Now,' he resumed, 'you are sure the robbery was not committed by anyone in your house?'

'Quite sure, sir.'

'Your key was never out of your possession?'

'Very rarely; and when I did not carry it, it was in one of the drawers in my desk.'

'Where was it on the evening of the robbery?'

'In my desk.'

'But then—'

'Excuse me, sir,' M. Fauvel interrupted, 'but may I mention that with a safe like mine the key counts for little. One must know the word at which to set the five movable buttons.'

'Did you tell anyone the word?'

'No, sir. Besides, Prosper changed the word when he felt so disposed. He used to tell me and I often forgot.'

'Had you forgotten it on the day of the robbery?'

'No; the word was changed the previous evening, and its strangeness struck me.'

'What was it?'

'Gypsy. G-y-p-s-y.' (The banker spelt it.)

This word M. Patrigent also wrote down.

'One more question, sir,' he said. 'Were you at home the evening of the robbery?'

'No, sir; I dined and spent the evening with a friend. When I returned, about one o'clock, my wife was in bed and I retired at once.'

'You are not aware of the sum of money in the safe?'

'No. My orders were that only a small sum should be kept there.'

M. Patrigent was silent. The important fact to him seemed to be that the banker was not aware there was 350,000 francs in the safe, and Prosper exceeded his duty in withdrawing it from the bank. The conclusion seemed obvious.

Seeing that he was not to be asked any more questions, the banker considered it a good opportunity to say what he had on his mind.

'I consider myself above suspicion,' he began, 'but I shall not sleep in peace till the robbery is brought home to my cashier. The sum is quite a fortune, and I shall be glad if you will examine my business affairs and see that I have no object in robbing myself.'

'That will do, sir,' the magistrate interposed; 'sign your statement, please!'

After the banker had gone, the clerk remarked:

'It is a very obscure affair; if the cashier is firm and clever it will be difficult to convict him, I think.'

'Perhaps,' the magistrate replied, 'but I will examine the other witness.'

Number four witness was Lucien, M. Fauvel's eldest son. He was a fine fellow of twenty-two, who said he was very fond of Prosper and looked upon him as an honest man.

He said he could offer no explanation as to why Prosper should commit the theft. He was sure he did not gamble as much as people made out and did not live beyond his means.

With regard to his cousin Madeleine he said:

'I always thought Prosper loved Madeleine and would marry her. I always attributed Prosper's departure to a quarrel with her, but I felt sure they would make it up.'

Lucien signed his statement and withdrew.

Cavaillon was the next to be examined. He was in a pitiful state, but determined to repair the mistake he made the previous day if possible.

He did not exactly accuse M. Fauvel, but he said he was a friend of the cashier, and as sure of his innocence as of his own. But unfortunately he had no evidence to support his statement.

Six or eight of the bank staff also made statements, but they were not important.

One of them gave a detail which the magistrate noted. He made out that he knew that Prosper had made a good deal of money on the Stock Exchange through M. Raoul de Lagors.

After the witnesses had concluded M. Patrigent sent the usher to find Fanferlot, which he did after some delay. The detective gave an account of the incident of the letter, which he was able to produce, having stolen it from Madame Gypsy, and furnished a number of biographical details he had gathered concerning Prosper and Madame Gypsy.

At the conclusion of the detective's story M. Patrigent murmured:

'Evidently the young man is guilty.'

This was not Fanferlot's opinion, and he was pleased to think the magistrate was upon the wrong track.

After he had furnished all the information possible, the detective was dismissed, the magistrate telling him to keep a careful eye upon Madame Gypsy as she probably knew something about the money.

The next day the magistrate took the evidence of Madame Gypsy and recalled M. Fauvel and Cavaillon. Only two of the witnesses who had been summoned failed to appear; the first was the messenger Prosper sent to the bank, who was ill, and M. Raoul de Lagors.

CHAPTER V

THE first two days of his imprisonment had not seemed very long to Prosper. He had been provided with writing materials and drawn up his defence. After that he became impatient at not being re-examined.

On Monday morning the door of his cell opened and his father, an old man with white hair, entered.

Prosper went forward to embrace him, but his father repulsed him.

'Keep away,' he said.

'You, too,' Prosper cried. 'You believe me to be guilty.'

'Spare me this shameful comedy,' his father interrupted, 'I know everything.'

'But, father, I am innocent, I swear it by my mother's sacred memory.'

'Wretch,' M. Bertomy cried, 'do not blaspheme! I am glad your mother is dead, Prosper, for your crime would have killed her.'

There was a long silence and then Prosper said:

'You overwhelm me, father, when I need all my courage and am the victim of an odious plot.'

'The victim!' said M. Bertomy. 'Are you making insinuations against your employer, the man who has done so much for you? It is bad enough to rob him; do not slander him. Was it a lie, too, when you wrote and told me to prepare to come to Paris, and ask M. Fauvel for his niece's hand for you?'

'No,' Prosper said in a faint voice.

'That is a year ago,' his father continued, 'and yet the thought of her could not keep you from bad companions and crime.'

'But, father, I love her still; let me explain—'

36

'That is enough, sir. I have seen your employer and know all about it. I have also seen the magistrate, and he gave me permission to visit you. I have seen your rooms and their luxury, and I can understand the reason of your crime; you are the first thief in the family.'

M. Bertomy, seeing his son was no longer listening to him, stopped.

'But,' he continued, 'I am not come to reproach you. Listen to me. How much have you left of the 350,000 francs you have stolen?'

'Once more, father, I am innocent.'

'I expected that reply. Now it rests with your relatives to repair your fault. The day I learned of your crime, your brother-in-law brought me your sister's dowry, 70,000 francs. I have 140,000 francs besides, making 210,000 francs in all. This I am going to hand to M. Fauvel.'

This statement roused Prosper.

'Don't do that!' he cried.

'I shall do so before night. M. Fauvel will give me time in which to pay the balance. My pension is 1,500 francs and I can live on 500. I am still strong enough to obtain employment.'

M. Bertomy said no more, stopped by his son's expression of anger.

'You have no right, father,' he cried, 'to do this. You can refuse to believe me if you like; but an action like that would ruin me. I am upon the edge of a precipice and you want to push me over. While justice hesitates, father, you condemn me without a hearing.'

Prosper's tones at last made an impression upon his father, who murmured:

'But the evidence against you is very strong.'

'That does not matter,' Prosper replied; 'I will prove myself innocent or perish in the attempt, whether I am convicted or not. The author of my misfortune is in the house of M. Fauvel and I will find him. Why did Madeleine tell me one day to think no more of her? Why did she exile me, when she loves me as much as I do her?'

The hour granted for the interview had expired. M. Bertomy left his son almost convinced of his innocence. Father and son embraced with tears in their eyes.

The door of Prosper's cell reopened almost immediately after his father's departure and the warder entered to conduct him to his examination. This time he went with his head high and a firm step.

As he passed through the room where the detectives and police were, the man with the gold spectacles said:

'Be brave, M. Bertomy, if you are innocent we will help you.'

Prosper, in surprise, asked the warder who the gentleman was. The warder replied:

'Surely you know the great Lecoq! If your case had been in his hands instead of Fanferlot's it would have been settled long ago. But he seems to know you.'

'I never saw him till I saw him here.'

'Don't be too sure of that, for he is a master of disguises.'

This time Prosper did not have to wait upon the wooden bench. M. Patrigent had arranged for his examination to immediately follow his interview with his father, with the object of getting the truth from him while his nerves were still vibrating with emotion.

The magistrate was, therefore, very surprised at the cashier's proud and resolute attitude.

The first question was:

'Have you reflected?'

'Being innocent,' Prosper replied, 'I have nothing on which to reflect.'

'Ah,' the magistrate said, 'you forget that sincerity and repentance are necessary to obtain lenient treatment.'

'I have need, sir, neither of pardon or leniency.'

'How would you answer,' the magistrate resumed, 'if I told you what had become of the money?'

Prosper shook his head sadly. 'In that case,' he said, 'I should not be here.'

The ordinary method of examination employed by the magistrate often succeeds, but it did not do so in this case.

'Then you persist in accusing your employer?'

'Either him or someone else.'

'Excuse me, it could only be he. No one else knew the word. Had he any reason to rob himself?'

'I know of none, sir.'

'Ah, well,' the magistrate said, 'I will tell you the reason you had to rob him.'

This was the magistrate's last effort to break through the cashier's calm and determined resistance.

'Will you tell me,' the magistrate began, 'how much you spent last year?'

Prosper answered promptly: 'About 50,000 francs.'

'Where did you get the money?'

'I inherited 12,000 francs from my mother. My salary and commission came to 14,000. I made about 8,000 on the Stock Exchange, and the rest I borrowed. I can repay the latter item as I have 15,000 francs to my credit with M. Fauvel.'

'Who lent you the money?'

'M. Raoul de Lagors.'

This gentleman had gone away on the day of the robbery, so he could not be examined.

'Now, tell me,' the magistrate said, 'what made you withdraw the money from the bank the day before it was required?'

'Because M. de Clameran gave me to understand, sir, that he required the money early in the morning.'

'Was he a friend of yours, then?'

'No, I did not like him, but he was a friend of M. de Lagors.'

'How did you spend the evening of the robbery?' the magistrate asked.

'After leaving the office at five, I went by train to Saint Germain and to M. Raoul de Lagors' country house with

1,500 francs he required. As he was not at home I left the money with the servant.'

'Did you know M. de Lagors was going to travel?'

'No, I do not know whether he is in Paris or not.'

'What did you do when you left your friend's house?'

'I returned to Paris and dined with a friend at a Boulevard restaurant.'

'After that?'

Prosper hesitated.

'As you won't say,' M. Patrigent went on, 'I will tell you how you spent your time. You went to the Rue Chaptal, dressed and went to a party given by a woman named Wilson, one of those women who disgrace the theatres by calling themselves dramatic artistes.'

'That is quite right, sir.'

'There is a good deal of play there, is there not?'

'Sometimes.'

'You frequent those kind of places, do you not? Were you not mixed up in a scandalous adventure with a woman of that class named Crescenzi?'

'I thought I was giving evidence concerning a robbery.'

'Yes, gambling leads to robbery. Did you not lose 1,800 francs at the woman Wilson's?'

'Excuse me, sir, only 1,100 francs.'

'Very well. In the morning you paid a bill of 1,000 francs.'

'Yes, sir.'

'Besides, there was 500 francs in your desk and 400 francs in your purse when you were arrested. In all that was 4,500 francs in twenty-four hours.'

Prosper was stupefied at this exact information which had been obtained in so short a time. At last he said:

'Your information is accurate, sir.'

'Where did this money come from, seeing that the previous evening you were so short you put off paying a small bill?'

'Sir, on the day you mention, I sold through an agent some securities for 3,000 francs and drew 2,000 francs salary in advance. I have nothing to hide.'

M. Patrigent renewed the attack from another point.

'If you have nothing to hide,' he said, 'why did you mysteriously pass this note to a colleague?'

The blow struck home. Prosper's eyes dropped before the magistrate's searching gaze.

'I thought, I wished—' he muttered.

'You wanted to conceal your mistress.'

'Yes, sir, that is true. I knew that when a man is accused of a crime, all the weaknesses of his life become evidence against him.'

'You mean the presence of a woman would give weight to the charge. You live with a woman?'

'I am young, sir.'

'Justice can pardon passing indiscretions, but cannot excuse the scandal of these unions. The man who respects himself so little as to live with a fallen woman does not raise the woman up to him, but he descends to her.'

'Sir.'

'I suppose you know who this woman is to whom you have loaned your mother's honourable name?'

'Madame Gypsy was a governess when I met her; she was born at Oporto and came to France with a Portuguese family.'

The magistrate shrugged his shoulders.

'Her name is not Gypsy,' he said, 'she has never been a governess, and she is not Portuguese.'

Prosper tried to protest, but M. Patrigent silenced him, and began searching through a number of documents.

'Ah, here it is; listen. Palmyre Chocareille, born at Paris in 1840, the daughter of Jacques Chocareille and Caroline Piedlent his wife. Palmyre Chocareille at the age of twelve was apprenticed to a bootmaker and stayed there till she was sixteen. At the age of seventeen she went as domestic servant to the Dombas, grocers, Rue Saint Denis, and stayed there three months. In that year, 1857, she had eight or ten places. In 1858, being weary of service, she went to work for a fan merchant in Passage Choiseul.'

The magistrate watched Prosper's face as he read to see the effect.

'At the end of 1858,' he continued, 'the girl Chocareille entered the service of a lady named Nunès and went with her to Lisbon. In 1861 she was in Paris again, and was sentenced at the Seine Court to three months imprisonment for wounding. She brought back the name of Nina Gypsy from Portugal.'

'But, sir,' Prosper began, 'I assure you—'

'Yes, I understand this story is not as romantic as the one she told you, but it is true. Six months after coming out of prison she made the acquaintance of a commercial traveller named Caldas, who was captivated by her beauty and who took rooms for her near the Bastille. She was living with him in his name till she left him for you. Have you ever heard of Caldas?'

'Never, sir.'

'This poor fellow loved her so madly that at the news of her departure he went mad with grief. He swore to kill the man who took her away, but he is supposed to have committed suicide, for after selling the furniture of the rooms he disappeared. That is the woman, your companion, for whom you stole. At least, admit that this woman was the cause of your downfall.'

'I could not do that, sir, for it is not the case.'

'At any rate she has been a great expense to you. Stop'—the magistrate drew out a bill—'last December you paid her dressmaker 2,000 francs.'

'All this money was spent willingly by me upon her.'

'You deny the evidence,' the magistrate continued. 'Do you deny that this girl was the cause of your changed habits?'

'Yes, sir, I do.'

'Then why did you suddenly disappear from a house where you were courting a young lady?'

'I cannot tell you my reasons,' Prosper replied.

The magistrate breathed more freely. He had found a weak spot in the prisoner's armour.

'Did Mademoiselle Madeleine dismiss you?' he asked.

Prosper was silent.

'Speak,' M. Patrigent insisted, 'I must warn you this is a very serious point.'

'However dangerous silence may be to me I shall not speak.'

The magistrate waited in silence for a further statement, which he did not receive, and then resumed:

'You have spent 50,000 francs in a year and exhausted your resources; you could not continue your kind of life; what did you think of doing?'

'I had no plans, sir.'

'You went on as long as you could and then drew upon your employer's safe?'

'Ah, sir, if I were guilty, I should not be here now. I should not have returned to my office.'

M. Patrigent could not prevent a smile of satisfaction as he said:

'I expected that argument. In remaining you showed your wisdom. Several recent cases have proved the futility of flight. Like a wise man you remained and said to yourself: "If the worst comes to the worst, after I have served my sentence I can enjoy the spoil." Many people would sacrifice five years of their life for 350,000 francs.'

'But, sir, if I had thought like that, I should have waited and taken a million.'

'Oh,' M. Patrigent said, 'it is not always possible to wait.'

After a few moments' thought, Prosper said:

'A detail has just come into my mind which may assist me. When the messenger brought the money from the bank, I was ready to leave, and I am sure I locked up the banknotes in his presence.'

'He shall be examined,' M. Patrigent said. 'You will be taken back to your cell.'

As soon as Prosper had gone, the magistrate turned to the clerk and said:

'Was not a medical certificate received to excuse the messenger Antonin's attendance? Where does he live?'

'Sir,' Sigault replied, 'he is at present in the Dubois Hospital.'

'Ah, well, I will go and examine him today. Send for a carriage.'

On reaching the hospital and finding the man well enough to be examined, M. Patrigent and his clerk went to his bedside.

When the messenger had answered the usual questions and said that he was Antonin Poche, that he was forty years old, was born at Cadaujac and a single man, the magistrate said:

'Are you well enough to answer my questions?'

'Quite, sir.'

'Did you go to the bank on February 27 to withdraw the 350,000 francs which were stolen?'

'Yes, sir.'

'What time did you return?'

'Rather late; it must have been five o'clock when I got back.'

'Do you remember what M. Bertomy did when you gave him the money? Now, think carefully.'

'First he counted the notes and made them up into four packets which he put in the safe, then locked the safe, yes, and I am quite sure of it, and went out.'

'Are you quite sure of what you are saying?' asked the magistrate.

The solemn tone of M. Patrigent frightened him.

'Sure,' he replied with marked hesitation, 'I would wager my head upon it.'

He would say no more for fear of being compromised, and it would not have taken much to make him withdraw his statement altogether.

As the magistrate went out he said to his clerk:

'It is becoming very serious.'

CHAPTER VI

THE *Grand-Archange Hôtel*, the refuge of Madame Gypsy, is the finest on the Quai Saint-Michel.

Madame Alexandré, the proprietress, once a beautiful woman, had become too big, though her eyes were still bright and her teeth white, but alas her nose was red.

She adored her husband, and just when M. Patrigent was leaving the Hospital she was waiting dinner for him.

Fanferlot himself appeared. They had met three years before, when she employed him as a private inquiry agent. They got married and with their joint savings took and furnished the *Grand-Archange Hôtel*, where they prospered and were esteemed. Fanferlot's employment in the detective service was kept a secret.

'How late you are,' she said as she kissed him.

'I am worn out,' he said; 'I have been playing billiards all day with Evariste, M. Fauvel's valet, and he won as often as he liked; he is a fellow who has no knowledge of anything but billiards. I made his acquaintance the day before yesterday and now I am his best friend. I am sure of his support if I apply for Antonin's berth as messenger.'

'What, you a messenger!'

'Yes, I must take the position to make inquiries there.'

'Did not the valet tell you anything?'

'Nothing of much use. The banker is a saint. He has no vices. He does not drink, gamble or keep a mistress. He is enormously rich and lives frugally. He loves his wife and children; he often has visitors but rarely goes out.'

'How old is his wife?'

'About fifty.'

'Have you found out,' Madame Alexandré asked, 'about the other members of the family?'

'Oh, yes. The younger son is an officer somewhere. The elder, Lucien, lives with his parents and is a model of virtue. I have found out nothing about the wife or the niece.'

'Do you know what I would do if I were in your place?'

'No.'

'I would consult M. Lecoq.'

The name made Fanferlot jump.

'That is fine advice,' he said. 'I should lose my position if he even suspected what I was doing.'

'I mean, ask his advice in an offhand way.'

'Perhaps you are right,' the detective said, 'but he is very clever and might guess. I will think it over. But how about Madame Nina Gypsy?'

The poor girl by coming to stay at the *Grand-Archange Hôtel* thought she was acting upon good advice and following Prosper's instructions. When she received a summons from M. Patrigent she admired the quickness of the police in finding her hiding-place, especially as she was staying there in her real name of Palmyre Chocareille.

'The girl is still upstairs,' Madame Alexandré replied, 'and suspects nothing. I do not know what the magistrate said to her, but she came back in a terrible rage, and wanted to go and see M. Fauvel and make a scene. Then she wrote a letter and gave it to Jean to post. Here it is.'

The letter was addressed to

Monsieur L. DE CLAMERAN,
Ironmaster,
Hôtel du Louvre.
To forward to M. Raoul de Lagors (very urgent).

Fanferlot unfastened the letter with great skill and read:

'M. RAOUL,
    'Prosper is in prison accused of a robbery which I am sure he has not committed. I wrote to you three days ago about it—'

'How could she have written without me seeing the letter?' Fanferlot interrupted. 'She must have posted it when she went to the Court.'

He went on reading:

'I have already written to you and received no reply. Who will come to Prosper's aid if his best friends abandon him? If you leave this letter without reply, I shall consider myself freed from my promise and, without a scruple, I shall tell Prosper the conversation between you and M. de Clameran I overheard. But I can rely upon you, can't I? I shall expect you at the *Hôtel Grand-Archange* between midday and four o'clock tomorrow.

'NINA GYPSY.'

Fanferlot at once proceeded to copy the letter and then put it back in its envelope. The porter opened the door and made a sign, and Fanferlot had only just time to disappear into a room at the back when Madame Gypsy entered.

She was very much changed. Her face was pale, her cheeks hollow and she had dark circles round her eyes.

Madame Alexandré was very surprised to see her and said: 'Are you going out, my child?'

'I must, madame, and I came to ask you, if anyone comes to see me, to tell them to wait.'

'Where are you going at this time, ill as you are?'

'I have received this note,' Madame Gypsy replied, 'read it!'

Madame Alexandré read this out very loud, so that Fanferlot could hear:

'A friend of Prosper who cannot receive you nor call upon you wishes to speak to you. This evening, Monday, at nine o'clock sharp, be in the omnibus booking office facing the tower of Saint Jacques and the writer will approach you and tell you what he has to say.

'I make the appointment there so that you will not feel afraid.'

'Are you going to keep the appointment?' cried Madame Alexandré.

'Certainly!'

'But it is terribly imprudent of you.'

'That does not matter, madame,' she said, as she walked out.

Before she was in the street Fanferlot had rushed furiously from his hiding-place.

'Is the *Grand-Archange* a public thoroughfare, then,' he cried, 'for a commissionaire to come without anyone seeing him?'

He seized a wig and a thick beard and disguised himself as a workman.

'I am going to follow her,' he said, 'and find out what she is concealing. Post that letter to M. de Clameran.'

Although Madame Gypsy had nearly ten minutes start on him, the detective soon overtook her, and followed her into the omnibus office. Just at nine o'clock, a man entered and went straight to Madame Gypsy and sat down by her side.

He was a man of medium height with fair whiskers and well but not noticeably dressed.

Fanferlot made up his mind to follow him and find out who he was. Unfortunately he could hear absolutely nothing of their conversation and had to be content with watching the expression of their faces.

The young woman's first look was one of surprise, then she half rose with a look of fear. She was soon reassured, but as the gentleman spoke she displayed some apprehension. She made a negative gesture but gave way before a good reason. At one moment she seemed ready to cry, at the next to laugh.

Just as Fanferlot was thinking of trying to get nearer to them, the gentleman rose and offered Madame Gypsy his arm and they went out.

He saw them get into a cab and he got ready for a long run.

When the cab got as far as the Boulevard Saint Denis, the detective felt a pain in his side, which compelled him to hang on behind the cab. At last it stopped outside a wine-shop and the driver went inside. The detective took up a position in a doorway to watch the occupants get out.

After waiting five minutes without seeing them, Fanferlot cautiously approached the cab, only to find it empty.

After the detective had recovered from the shock he came to the conclusion that they must have got in by one door of the cab and out by the other, to prevent being followed. He decided to make inquiries of the driver; but he was in a very bad temper, shook his whip at him, and would tell him nothing.

Fanferlot sorrowfully wended his way back to the Quai Saint-Michel, where his first words were:

'Has the girl come back?'

'No,' was the reply, 'but two parcels have come for her.'

He skilfully opened the parcels and found they contained common dresses, skirts, thick shoes and linen bonnets— apparently a disguise.

On his way back Fanferlot had made up his mind to say nothing to his wife of his failure, but he changed his mind and told her the whole story.

Madame Gypsy did not return till one o'clock, and her first inquiry was whether anything had come for her.

Madame Alexandré replied in the affirmative, and asked whether she had seen M. Bertomy's friend.

'Yes, madame,' she replied, 'and his advice has so changed my plans that I shall be leaving you tomorrow.'

'Has anything happened, then?'

'Nothing which would interest you,' Madame Gypsy replied, as she lit her candle and retired.

After she had gone Fanferlot came out of the hiding-place where he had been while his wife was talking to Madame Gypsy, and they discussed the situation. Fanferlot decided to ask the advice of M. Lecoq the following day.

Early the following morning Fanferlot arrived at M. Lecoq's residence, but he was so nervous that he hardly had courage enough to ring the bell.

When the door was opened, the servant's first words to the detective were:

'Ah, you have come at the right time. The master expects you.'

After considerable hesitation Fanferlot allowed himself to be shown into the study, where he was greeted by M. Lecoq, who put down his pen and said:

'Ah, here you are, my boy. The Bertomy affair is not going on very well, is it? You have made a fine muddle of it.'

M. Lecoq got up, and turning suddenly on Fanferlot said in a hard and ironical voice:

'What do you think, Master Squirrel, of a man who abuses his employer's confidence, who reveals just enough of what he discovers to mislead the prosecution, and who betrays the cause of justice and that of the accused for his own vanity?'

Fanferlot drew back in fright and began:

'I would say—'

'You think this man should be punished, and you are right. The less a profession is honoured, the more honourable those who follow it should be.'

'But, sir, I swear—'

'Silence. Would you like to prove that you told the magistrate everything, as was your duty? While everyone is trying to convict the cashier you are working against the banker.'

Fanferlot could not make out whether M. Lecoq was really angry or not.

'You are quite right, sir,' he said piteously.

'You are not even clever,' M. Lecoq continued. 'Now, on the day you were first called upon to give evidence before the magistrate, you most probably—I do not say I am absolutely certain—had in your hands the means of finding out whose key opened the safe.'

'How?'

'You remember the scratch you so carefully examined through a glass? If you had examined the keys of the banker and his cashier carefully, you would probably have found some traces on the key with which the scratch was made.'

Fanferlot beat his brow fiercely and cried out, 'Fool that I am!'

'You are quite right,' M. Lecoq continued; 'you have neglected this most important clue. But sit down and tell me all you know of the affair.'

Fanferlot told the facts, but from a feeling of vanity omitted to mention how Madame Gypsy and the gentleman had outwitted him the previous evening, and when he had finished M. Lecoq said:

'It seems to me. Master Squirrel, you have forgotten something. How far did you follow the empty cab?'

Fanferlot blushed and said, 'What, do you know about that, sir, too?'

An idea suddenly struck him; he jumped out of his chair as he said:

'You were the gentleman with the fair whiskers.'

Fanferlot's surprise made his face look so funny that M. Lecoq could not repress a smile.

'Ah, sir,' continued the detective, 'what an actor you would make! But I was disguised, too!'

'Yes; very badly though. Do you think a thick beard and a blouse are a sufficient disguise? To change the appearance of the eyes is the great secret.'

That was the reason why the official Lecoq was never seen at the prefecture of police without his gold-rimmed spectacles.

'In that case,' Fanferlot continued, 'you know the reason why Madame Gypsy is leaving the *Grand-Archange* without waiting for M. de Clameran, and has bought a disguise?'

'She is acting upon my advice.'

'In that case,' the detective said, 'I am a fool.'

'No, Squirrel,' M. Lecoq continued, 'you are not a fool, but you have undertaken a task which is too much for you.'

Fanferlot was surprised to find his chief so affable now, and it made him a bit suspicious.

'Can you put your finger on the thief, sir?' he said.

'No more than you can, and I have not even formed an opinion as you have. The only thing of which I am sure is the scratch on the safe door.'

As he spoke, M. Lecoq pulled out a photograph of the safe door, which showed everything, including the scratch, very clearly.

'Here is the scratch,' he said. 'It runs from top to bottom, starting from the keyhole, diagonally, and from left to right; that is to say, it terminates by the door of the staircase leading to the banker's apartments. It is very deep near the keyhole and ends in a hardly visible mark.'

'I see that, sir.'

'You naturally thought it was made by the thief. Here is a little safe like M. Fauvel's. Take a key and try to scratch it.'

The detective did as he was told, and after rubbing the end of a key upon it said:

'This paint is very hard.'

'And the paint on the safe is harder still. So you see, the scratch on the safe was not made by the key slipping in the thief's trembling hand. I spent three days trying to understand the scratch, and only succeeded yesterday.'

M. Lecoq went to the door of his bedroom, took out the key and held it in his hand.

'Come here,' he said to Fanferlot; 'stand by my side. Suppose I want to open the door and you want to prevent me. When you see me attempt to put the key in the lock what is your instinctive movement?'

'I put my two hands upon your arm and draw it quickly towards me, so that you cannot put in the key.'

'Then do so.'

Fanferlot obeyed, and the key M. Lecoq held turned from the lock, slid along the door, and traced a sharp scratch from top to bottom, just like the one in the photograph.

Fanferlot was speechless with surprise.

'Do you see now?' asked M. Lecoq.

'Yes, sir, I do. A child could understand now. There must have been at the time of the robbery two persons near the safe: one trying to take the notes, the other trying to prevent it.'

'You go too far,' M. Lecoq said; 'you are accepting as a fact something which is only a probability.'

'No, sir; no,' Fanferlot cried; 'a man like you does not make a mistake.'

'What then does our discovery prove?'

'First, that the cashier is innocent.'

'Why?'

'Because he was free to open the safe when he pleased and would not have committed the theft in the presence of a witness.'

'Yes, quite so; but the same argument applies to the banker, who is innocent too.'

'Quite true,' said Fanferlot after a moment's reflection. 'What is to be done now?'

'Look for the other person, the one who took the notes, and who is quite at his ease while others are suspected.'

'But M. Fauvel and his cashier were the only two who had keys.'

'On the evening of the robbery the banker left his key in his desk.'

'The key is not sufficient to open the safe. It is necessary to know the word too.'

M. Lecoq shrugged his shoulders and asked:

'What was the word?'

'Gypsy.'

'The name of the cashier's mistress. When you can find a man sufficiently intimate with Prosper to guess the word, and familiar enough with M. Fauvel to obtain the entry into his bedroom, you will have found the real criminal.'

Fanferlot was surprised at his chief giving advice where he usually gave orders, so he asked him:

'Have you any personal interest, sir, in the case?'

'You were always very curious, Master Squirrel,' M. Lecoq replied,' but don't let your curiosity go too far. I am assisting you because it suits me to do so. I have reasons for not wishing to appear in this case, and I forbid you from mentioning my name in connection with it. If we succeed you will obtain the credit.'

'I will be discreet, sir,' the detective said.

'In the first place,' M. Lecoq said, 'take the photograph of the safe to M. Patrigent, who is, I know, very perplexed over the case. Explain the scratch to him as I did to you, give a demonstration to him, and I feel sure he will set the cashier at liberty. Prosper must be free for me to begin operations.'

'Am I to let the magistrate see that I suspect someone besides the cashier and the banker?'

'Of course. Tell him that you will keep your eye on Prosper.'

'And suppose he asks about Gypsy?'

After a moment's hesitation, M. Lecoq replied:

'Say that you have decided that she shall stay in a house where she can watch someone you suspect.'

Fanferlot was ready to go, but M. Lecoq detained him with a gesture:

'I have not done yet,' he said. 'Can you drive a carriage and look after a horse?'

'Of course I can, sir.'

'Then, when you have seen the magistrate, go home quickly, dress up as a valet and take this letter to the registry office keeper at the corner of Delorme Passage. He will introduce you to M. de Clameran, who wants a valet.'

'Excuse me, sir, but M. de Clameran does not fulfil the conditions. He is not the cashier's friend.'

'Do as I tell you,' said M. Lecoq sternly. 'M. Clameran is not Prosper's friend, but he is the protector of Raoul de

Lagors. What is the cause of the intimacy of these two men of such different ages? We must find out. We must find out, too, something about the ironmaster. He has a carriage which you must drive.'

'You shall be obeyed, sir.'

'One word more. M. de Clameran is a suspicious gentleman. You will take the name of Joseph Dubois, and here are three characters in that name. Keep your eyes open and be a good servant. But do not be too honest or you will arouse suspicion. I shall see you every day, but do not come here as you may be followed. If anything unforeseen happens send to your wife, and she will let me know.'

As the door closed behind Fanferlot, M. Lecoq went into his bedroom, and in a short time became the stout gentleman with the fair whiskers once more.

'Now,' he said to himself, 'I have not forgotten anything or left anything to chance.'

Fanferlot almost flew to the Palais de Justice. Here was a chance of displaying his perspicacity, or rather passing off someone else's as his own.

The magistrate was not absolutely convinced, but admired the ingenuousness of the theory, and told Fanferlot as he was leaving that the cashier would probably be released on the following day.

He began to draw up one of those terrible orders which give the accused his liberty but do not give him back his honour; which say he is not guilty but do not say he is innocent.

Turning to his clerk he said:

'This is another of those crimes where the criminals will never be brought to justice. One more dossier for the archives.'

He wrote upon the outside of the papers concerning the case the number: *Dossier, No.113*.

CHAPTER VII

AFTER nine days' imprisonment Prosper Bertomy on Thursday morning was liberated.

Acquittal after a trial is a rehabilitation, but this kind of freedom leaves an eternal suspicion. Prosper felt the horror of his position so keenly that his first thought was to commit suicide.

'No,' he said, 'I have no right to kill myself. Now, I will not die till I have established my innocence.'

Almost in despair he went towards his apartments. The thought that Nina Gypsy loved him and believed in him was very sweet, though he did not love her.

When he reached his rooms in the Rue Chaptal, the porter met him and offered his congratulations. Prosper cut short the painful subject by asking:

'Do you know where madame has gone?'

'No, sir,' the porter replied. 'She went away on the day of your arrest, and I have not seen her since.'

'Where are the servants?'

'Your father paid them, sir, and dismissed them,'

'Have you my key?'

'No, sir. When your father went away at eight this morning, he said he was leaving a great friend who was to be treated as master till your return. He is a stout man with fair whiskers.'

Prosper was very much astonished, but did not show it. He went upstairs and rang the bell. His father's friend opened the door.

'Charmed to make your acquaintance, sir,' he said.

He seemed to have made himself quite at home.

'You are surprised to see me here, are you not?' the stranger said. 'Your father wanted to introduce me, but he was obliged to go back to Beaucaire this morning. He is convinced of your innocence, and so am I. This letter he has left will, I hope, take the place of an introduction.'

After reading the letter, Prosper stretched out his hand to the stout gentleman.

'My father,' he said, 'tells me you are his best friend, and tells me to trust you and take your advice.'

'That is right. This morning your father said: "Verduret—that is my name—my son is in a scrape, we must help him out." Let us get to business. What do you think of doing?'

This question roused the cashier's anger.

'I mean to find the wretch who has ruined me, and hand him over to justice. That will be my vengeance.'

'Have you any means of doing so?'

'None. But I shall succeed, for a man who gives up his life is sure to succeed.'

'Well said, M. Prosper. I have formed a plan. In the first place you must sell your furniture, leave this house, and disappear.'

'Disappear,' cried the cashier. 'That would be acknowledging my guilt.'

'But you have an enemy, who can only be captured by his own imprudence, and as long as he can see you he will be afraid.'

'I will take your advice,' Prosper said after a few minutes' reflection.

'I was sure you would. Have you any money? No? Then the proceeds of the sale will be very useful. I was so sure of convincing you that I called in a dealer, who will give you 12,000 francs for everything except the pictures.'

The cashier winced, and this caused M. Verduret to say:

'Yes, I know it is hard, but it is necessary. But let us go on . . . You are a friend of M. de Lagors, are you not?'

'Yes, I am his intimate friend.'

'Who is he?'

'M. de Lagors,' Prosper answered in a somewhat offended tone, 'is M. Fauvel's nephew! He is a rich, distinguished and clever young man, as good and loyal as anyone I know.'

'I am glad,' said M. Verduret, 'that I am about to make the acquaintance of such a paragon, for I have taken the liberty of making an appointment with him here in your name.'

'What,' cried Prosper, 'you suppose—?'

'Oh, I suppose nothing. I want to see him.'

At that moment the bell rang.

'Where can I hide so that I can see and hear?'

'There, in my room; leave the door open.'

The bell rang a second time.

'On your life, Prosper,' M. Verduret said in most convincing tones, 'not a word about your plans or about me. Be weak, feeble, hesitating.'

Prosper opened the door to Raoul. He was a good-looking fellow of twenty-four, though he hardly looked twenty. He had curly auburn hair, an intelligent forehead, and frank blue eyes.'

His first movement was to fall upon the cashier's neck.

'Poor dear Prosper,' he said, though there appeared to be a little constraint in his manner. 'Your letter,' continued Raoul, 'quite upset me; I said to myself, Is he going mad? So I hastened here.'

Prosper was wondering what the letter he had not written contained.

'Don't give way; why despair?' he went on. 'You are young enough to begin life over again. I am rich, and half my fortune is at your disposal.'

This noble offer touched Prosper deeply.

'Thank you, Raoul,' he said. 'All the money in the world is of no use.'

'Why? What are your plans? Are you stopping in Paris?'

'I don't know; I have no plans.'

'You must begin life over again. You cannot remain in Paris as long as the robbery is not explained.'

'Suppose it is never explained?'

'All the more reason why you should be forgotten. I was talking to Clameran about you a little while ago. He said if he were in your place he would go to America, make a fortune, and come back and crush those who suspected him.'

'I will think it over,' the cashier said. 'But what does M. Fauvel say?'

'I have not seen him for a month, but I have heard of him through Cavaillon, and he is very upset. In fact, they say he is suffering from a terrible malady. Madame Fauvel and Madeleine are very well, though very busy preparing for the fancy-dress ball at the Jandidiers. But I shall have to go now. Prosper. Bear up, and whatever happens, remember you can count upon me.'

Raoul shook hands with Prosper and was in the street before the voice of the man with the fair whiskers roused the cashier from his meditations.

'Fine friends!' said M. Verduret. 'He might just as well have offered you the whole of his fortune while he was about it. Those promises are not binding. But I think he would cheerfully give 10,000 francs to know that the ocean was between you and him.'

'Why, sir; why?'

'Perhaps for the same reason that he told you he had not been to his uncle's for a month.'

'But now, if you will change your clothes, we will pay M. Fauvel a visit.'

'Never,' he cried; 'I could not bear the sight of him.'

'I am sorry,' said M. Verduret, 'but it is necessary. I must see M. Fauvel. Surely you can stand a five minutes' interview. I will pose as a relative of yours and you will not have a word to say.'

Prosper consented and had just gone into his room to dress when the bell rang again. M. Verduret opened the door and found the porter with a letter for M. Bertomy which he had forgotten in the morning.

The address of the letter was not written, but the words composing it were formed by letters cut from a book or paper and stuck on the envelope.

Telling the porter to wait, M. Verduret took the letter into the other room to Prosper and opened it. It contained ten thousand franc notes and a few words composed in the same way as the address. The words were:

'Dear Prosper, a friend who knows the horror of your position sends you this help. It comes from a heart which has shared your anguish. Leave France; you are young, and the future is yours. Go away, and may the money bring you happiness.'

As M. Verduret read this aloud Prosper's anger increased. 'Everyone wants me to go,' he said.

'Yes,' said M. Verduret with a smile; 'there are people who hate you for the wrong they have done you, and who would banish you at all costs. Your presence here is a menace to them.'

'Who are they, sir, tell me?'

'If I knew, my dear Prosper, I should know the thief. But we will find them. I have now got a fact which proves my deductions to be accurate. Let us take advantage of our enemies' imprudence, and we will begin by making inquiries of the porter.'

M. Verduret asked the porter if he knew who brought the letter. He replied that it was a commissionaire from the wine shop at the corner of the Rue Pigale, and he was at once sent to fetch him.

After satisfying himself, from their numbers, that the notes were not part of the stolen money, M. Verduret said:

'I feel sure these notes were not sent by the thief, and in that case they very likely came from the other person who was near the safe at the time and could not prevent the robbery.'

The cashier tried to follow this reasoning.

'Now,' the other man continued, 'we must look for this other person.'

He picked up the letter and read it three or four times slowly.

'Evidently,' he murmured, 'the letter was put together by a woman. A man sending another man money would never have used the word "help". A man would have said "a loan" or "funds". Only a woman ignorant of masculine susceptibilities would have used the word. The phrase, too, "It comes from a heart which has shared your anguish", could only have been conceived by a woman.'

Prosper interrupted with the remark:

'I think you are wrong; there was no woman mixed up in the affair;' but M. Verduret took no notice of the interruption.

'We must first try,' he continued, 'to find out from where the letters were cut.'

He went to the window and after a careful scrutiny, said:

'Small characters, delicate, clear, and well printed on good paper. So these words were not cut from a newspaper or an ordinary novel. But I have seen the characters and know them. Didot often uses similar ones, and so does Mame.' He stopped and then tapped his forehead.

'I have it,' he said. 'These words were cut from a prayer book.'

He moistened some of the words with his tongue, and on removing them found on the back of one the word 'God'.

'Now,' he said, 'what has become of the mutilated book? Was it burnt? No, a bound book does not burn in that state. It has been thrown into a corner.'

At that moment the porter arrived with the commissionaire.

'Ah,' said the stout man in his most genial way. 'Do you remember bringing this letter this morning?'

'Very well, sir. I noticed the address in particular. You don't often see one like it.'

'Who gave it you to deliver? Was it a man or a woman?'

'It was a commissionaire.'

'Do you know him?'

'No, sir.'

'What was he like?'

'He was of medium height and wore a vest of green velvet, and his badge—'

'That is rather vague. Did he tell you who sent him?'

'No, sir. He only gave me ten sous and said a cabman had given it to him on the Boulevard.'

This reply seemed to disconcert M. Verduret.

'Would you recognize,' he continued, 'the commissionaire if you saw him again?'

'Yes, sir.'

'Then how much do you earn a day as a commissionaire?'

'I hardly know, sir; from eight to ten francs, I should think.'

'Well, I will give you ten francs a day to walk about and look for the other commissionaire. Every evening you must come to the *Hôtel Grand-Archange* on the Quai Saint-Michel to report and get your pay. Ask for M. Verduret. If you find the man you shall have fifty francs. Does that suit you?'

'Yes, sir, that will suit me well.'

'Then do not lose a moment; off you go!'

Prosper began to understand the idea of M. Verduret's investigations, and to admire his resource.

'So,' he asked, when the commissionaire had gone, 'you think you have discovered a woman's hand in the affair?'

'Yes, and a devout one, too, who possessed two prayer-books and mutilated one to write to you. I have great hopes of finding her, too, thanks to the means I have of immediate search.'

He sat down and wrote a few lines, rolled up the paper and put it in his pocket.

'Are you ready for our visit to M. Fauvel? Come along, we have earned our lunch.'

CHAPTER VIII

Raoul de Lagors had not exaggerated when he said that M. Fauvel was suffering from extraordinary depression. The banker shut himself up in his private room and would see no one.

At three o'clock on the afternoon of Prosper's release a messenger entered his room and said that his former cashier and a relative wished to see him.

The banker jumped up, crying: 'How dare Prosper!'

But he realized that he must not give way to his feelings in front of his employee, so he said:

'Show the gentlemen in.'

If M. Verduret had counted upon a curious scene he was not disappointed. The banker's face was as red as if he were about to be seized with an attack of apoplexy, and Prosper was as livid as a corpse, as they gazed at one another with mortal hatred.

After a minute's silence, during which M. Verduret calmly examined these two enemies, he addressed the banker:

'You have doubtless heard, sir, of my relative's release.'

'Yes,' M. Fauvel replied, making praiseworthy efforts to contain himself; 'the evidence was not sufficient.'

'Quite so, sir; and because of that my relative is going to America.'

A look of relief spread over the banker's face.

'Oh, he is going away!' he said; and the way he said it was a mortal insult.

M. Verduret took no notice, but continued:

'Before leaving I wished him to pay his respects to his old employer.'

'M. Bertomy,' he replied, 'might have spared me this painful interview. I have nothing more to say.'

This was their dismissal, and M. Verduret went out dragging Prosper with him.

In the street the cashier recovered his speech. 'I have done as you wished, sir. I hope you are satisfied.'

'Yes,' M. Verduret replied. 'I could not see the banker without you, and I have satisfied myself that he is not concerned in the robbery.'

'But, sir, he might be pretending!'

'No, not to that extent. I also wanted to know whether he would be susceptible to certain suspicions. Now I can answer boldly "Yes".'

They had stopped to talk in the middle of an open space at the corner of the Rue Lafayette, and M. Verduret was looking round anxiously as if he expected someone. An exclamation of delight escaped him when he saw Cavaillon with a bare head running towards them.

Cavaillon was in such a hurry that he did not stop to congratulate Prosper but immediately addressed M. Verduret.

'They are gone,' he said.

'Long?'

'No, about a quarter of an hour.'

'Then we have no time to lose,' M. Verduret said as he gave Cavaillon the note he had written some time before; 'give him this and go back quickly, so that your absence is not noted.'

Cavaillon set off at a run. Prosper was surprised. He said:

'I did not know you were acquainted with Cavaillon. But where are we going now?'

'You shall soon see,' said M. Verduret, as he set off along the Rue Lafayette, as far as number 81, at top speed.

'We will go in here,' he said to Prosper.

They went up to the second floor and stopped before a door which had 'millinery' upon it. M. Verduret tapped with his fingers and the door was opened at once by a well-dressed woman of about forty, who bowed respectfully before them.

M. Verduret gave her a questioning glance, to which she replied:

'Yes.'

'In there?' said M. Verduret, pointing to a door.

'No,' the woman replied, 'in the small drawing-room on the other side.'

M. Verduret opened the door indicated and gently pushed Prosper inside, saying as he did so:

'Go in and keep cool.'

His first glance caused him to cry out:

'Madeleine!'

M. Fauvel's niece, more beautiful than ever, was standing in the centre of the room. She had come to try on her dress as Maid of Honour to Catherine de Medici, which she was to wear at the fancy dress ball, and her surprise was so great that she almost fainted.

Her weakness only lasted for a moment, and then her eyes, which at first were so tender, expressed nothing but pride and resentment.

'How dare you, sir,' she said, 'spy upon me and follow me here. You swore upon your honour never to seek me out. Is this how you keep your word?'

'I took that oath, mademoiselle, but so much has happened since. It was not my own design which brought me here. I did not think you would repulse me in my misfortune.'

Prosper could see the struggle which was taking place in her, but she replied in a steady voice:

'You know me well enough, Prosper, to know that I pity you as a sister pities a beloved brother.'

'What have I done,' said Prosper bitterly, 'to be dismissed as I was after three years' happiness?'

'I told you to forget,' she murmured.

'Forget!' Prosper said. 'How can I forget? Can I stop the circulation of my blood?'

They were interrupted by a sob from Madeleine's maid, whose presence they had forgotten. Prosper looked at her, and though she was dressed as a maid she was Nina Gypsy.

Prosper was so horrified at the situation that he could not speak. He was between the two women who had decided his life; he loved one of them and was adored by the other. He was astonished, too, that Gypsy was weeping without making any protest or reviling him.

During the time that Prosper was silent Madeleine recovered her composure and prepared to depart. When she was ready to go she said:

'Why did you come? We both of us need all our courage, for we are both unhappy and I am more so even than you. A day will perhaps come when I shall be able to justify myself. Goodbye, my only friend, goodbye.'

She leant towards Prosper, kissed him on the forehead and went out, followed by Nina Gypsy.

Prosper seemed as if he had awakened out of a dream. A feeling of wonder took possession of him. Who could this marvellous man be who seemed to arrange events to suit himself? When M. Verduret entered, Prosper's first words were:

'Who are you?'

'A friend of your father's,' was the reply he received.

Prosper told him that the reason he wished to defend his honour was that some day Madeleine might come back to him. But after that interview there seemed no chance and that he would give up the struggle.

Prosper's resolution seemed to alarm M. Verduret, who said:

'I must apologize for listening to your interview, but the end will justify the means. Do you not suspect anything? Did you not understand her words? Take courage, Prosper, Mademoiselle Madeleine loves you and has never ceased to do so.'

'Oh, if I could only think so!'

'Believe me, for I am not mistaken. You did not understand as I did her sufferings in her struggle between her love and what she believes to be her duty.'

At these words Prosper's hope and confidence came back. M. Verduret continued:

'Why do you shut your eyes to evidence? Don't you understand that Madeleine knows the thief's name?'

'Impossible!'

'It is true. But no human power can tear it from her. She is sacrificing you, but she first sacrificed herself.'

'Alas!' Prosper cried as he clasped M. Verduret's hand, 'you must think me very stupid, but you do not know how I suffer.'

'I have suffered too, just as you have suffered,' the man with the fair whiskers said, with tears in his eyes.

Prosper was silent for a moment, and then said:

'I have decided, sir; my honour is a sacred trust. I am ready to do as you order.'

The same day Prosper sold his furniture and wrote to his friends to tell them of his immediate departure to San Francisco. In the evening he took up his quarters at the *Hôtel Grand-Archange*.

About eleven o'clock that night he opened his window, but a gust of wind shook the curtains and blew a piece of paper about the room.

Prosper mechanically picked up the paper and found it covered with Nina Gypsy's writing.

It was a piece of a torn letter and read:

'from M. Raoul, I have been . . .
'a plot against him . . .
'warn Prosper and then . . .
'hand of Mademoiselle Ma . . .'

Prosper had no sleep that night.

CHAPTER IX

THERE is a little café in the Rue Saint-Honoré called the *Bonne Foi*. M. Verduret had made an appointment here with Prosper on the following day for four o'clock, when it would be practically deserted. After he had ordered a chop and the waiter had disappeared, he said:

'Well, Prosper, have you carried out my instructions?'

'Yes, sir.'

'Have you seen the costumier?'

'Yes, I gave him your letter and everything will be sent to the *Grand-Archange*.'

'Very well! I have some good news. While we are waiting for those of our emissaries with whom I have made appointments here, let us pay a little attention to M. de Lagors.'

'Do you know from what part of the country he comes?' asked M. Verduret.

'From Madame Fauvel's district, Saint Rémy.'

'Are you sure?'

'Oh, quite sure, sir. I have heard him say so a hundred times.'

'That is very singular,' said M. Verduret.

'What is that, sir?' Prosper asked.

'Saint Rémy is a very charming place, but it is not your friend's birthplace.'

'But I have proofs, sir.'

'They are not genuine. While you were in prison I wrote to Saint Rémy and received replies. Here is No. 1.'

He read:

'Lagors, a very old family, originally from Mailano, but residing at Saint Rémy for a hundred years.

69

'The last of the Lagors (Jules René Henri), bearing, without any clearly defined rights, the title of Count married in 1829, Rosalie Clarisse Fontanet, of Tarascon; he died in December, 1848, without an heir, leaving only two girls. There is no mention of any person of the name in the registers of the district.'

Prosper was astounded.

'Why does M. Fauvel treat Raoul as a nephew?' he said.

'As his wife's nephew, you mean. But let us look at the second answer.'

'Jules René Henri Lagors, the last of his name, died at Saint Rémy on December 29, 1848, in a state of misery. He had a small fortune, but silkworm-farming had ruined him.

'He did not leave a son, but two daughters, one of whom is a governess at Aix, and the other is married to a merchant from Orgen. His widow lives upon the liberality of a relative, the wife of a rich banker in the Capital. No one of the name of Lagors is known in the district of Arles.'

'That is all. But I think it is enough. Some people might say that perhaps the widow of Lagors, after her husband's death, had a natural son, who was not acknowledged but bore his name. This objection is overcome by your friend's age. Raoul is twenty-four, and it is less than twenty years since M. de Lagors died.'

'Who can he be?' asked Prosper.

'I do not know, and that will be much more difficult to discover. One person could tell us but he would not do so.'

'Is it M. de Clameran?'

'Quite right.'

'He always inspired me with a feeling of repulsion.'

'I have a few notes about him which your father supplied, but I am expecting some others.'

'What did my father say?'
'Nothing in his favour. Listen.'

'Louis de Clameran was born at the Château de Clameran near Tarascon. He had an elder brother named Gaston. In 1842, after an affray in which he had the misfortune to kill one man and seriously injure another, Gaston was obliged to go abroad. He was a frank, loyal, honourable fellow, loved by everybody. Louis, on the contrary, had most detestable ways and was hated.

'After his father's death Louis went to Paris, and in less than two years got through, not only his own share of his father's property, but also his exiled brother's.

'At last, overwhelmed with debt, Louis de Clameran went as a soldier. On leaving the service he was lost sight of; it is only known that he lived in England and in Germany.

'In 1865 we find him back in Paris. He was in the utmost distress and frequented the worst society.

'He was reduced to the most shameful expedients, when he heard of his brother's return. Gaston had made a fortune in Mexico. He was still young and used to an active life, so he purchased near Oloron an iron foundry. Directly afterward, that is six months ago, he died in his brother Louis' arms. His death gave our Clameran a large fortune and the title of marquis.'

Prosper reflected, and then said:
'From that it seems that M. de Clameran was in profound misery when I saw him for the first time at M. Fauvel's. Shortly after that Lagors arrived from the provinces, and about a month afterwards Madeleine suddenly dismissed me.'
'Come,' said M. Verduret, 'I see you are beginning to understand the significance of facts.'
He stopped as a fresh customer entered the *Bonne Foi*. The newcomer was dressed as a servant in a good

family. After a rapid glance round he made straight for M. Verduret.

'Ah, well, Master Joseph Dubois,' said the fat man.

Prosper's attention was fixed upon the smart servant whose face seemed familiar to him, and who sat down at the next table and ordered a glass of absinthe.

'I must say,' the servant began, 'my job is not an easy one. Yesterday my master went out. I followed him and he went to the *Grand-Archange* to see the little lady. On finding out she had gone, he rushed back home, where Raoul de Lagors was waiting for him. The latter asked him what was the matter, and he replied that the woman had gone, she had slipped through their fingers. Then Lagors asked: "Does she know anything serious?" Clameran replied: "she only knows what I told you, but it is sufficient to put anyone on the right track." Lagors turned pale and said: "If it is so serious we must get rid of her." My master only laughed and shrugged his shoulders as he said: "It is easy enough to get rid of a woman of her class with the help of the law." This idea made them both laugh.'

'The idea is a good one,' M. Verduret said, 'but it is too late to carry it out.'

Prosper listened to the report with feverish curiosity. He thought now he could understand the fragment of Gypsy's letter.

Master Joseph continued:

'Yesterday, after dinner, my master, after dressing most carefully, called upon M. Fauvel and stayed all the evening.'

'What!' cried Prosper; 'after his insulting remarks on the day of the robbery?'

'How did he look when he came away?' M. Verduret asked.

'Not very well pleased I am sure, for when I knocked at his door to know if he wanted anything he cursed me through the door.'

'This morning,' master Joseph went on, 'he got up in a bad temper. At midday Raoul called and they started quarrelling.

My master had him by the throat and did not let go till Raoul drew a knife. They spoke English, so I could not understand what they were saying. After they cooled down they talked in French again, on unimportant subjects, till Raoul was leaving, when my master said to him: "Since this scene is inevitable and it takes place today, stay at home at Vésinet this evening". Raoul replied: "I will".'

It was now getting dark, and the café was filling up.

'You must go,' M Verduret said to Joseph, 'your master may want you. Here is someone who wants to speak to me.'

This time it was Cavaillon, who seemed more troubled and nervous than ever. He sat down at another table and after taking precautions that he was not observed, he handed M. Verduret a small packet, saying:

'This she found in a cupboard.'

It was a richly bound prayer-book, from which words, corresponding to the letter Prosper had received, were missing.

Prosper turned pale at the sight of the book and said:

'It belongs to Madeleine. I gave it to her. It had her name, too, upon the title page.'

M. Verduret got up to meet a young man who had just come in, and who gave him a note. He had hardly glanced at it when he called out in a state of great excitement.

'Perhaps we shall catch them now!' He dragged Prosper outside, and picking out a well-horsed carriage, asked the driver what the charge would be to drive to Vésinet.

'I don't know the way,' the cabman replied.

Prosper volunteered to show him the way, and M. Verduret offering him a hundred francs if he could overtake a carriage which had half an hour's start, he set off at a gallop.

CHAPTER X

THE driver earned his hundred francs, and when M. Verduret and Prosper got out of the carriage at Vésinet, they could see the lamps of the other carriage just in front of them.

It was raining in torrents and pitch dark as they ran along the road till they reached the gate of Raoul's house, outside which the other carriage was standing.

M. Verduret made an attempt to obtain information from the driver of this carriage as to his passengers, but the man who was half asleep upon his box seemed to think that M. Verduret and Prosper were thieves, and threatened to call for help if they did not go away.

Not daring to enter the garden of the house by the gate, they crept along outside the wall, which was ten or twelve feet high, looking for a place to climb over.

Fortunately M. Verduret though fat was nimble, and succeeded with a tremendous leap in grasping the top of the wall. He soon pulled himself up the wall and was able to help Prosper.

The house in which M. de Lagors lived was built in the middle of a large garden. It was a narrow house, two storeys high, and there was a light in a room on the second floor.

'You know the house,' M. Verduret said to Prosper; 'where is the light?'

'In Raoul's bedroom.'

'What rooms are there on the ground floor?'

'The kitchen, the dining-room and the billiard-room.'

'On the first floor?'

'Two drawing-rooms, joined by folding doors, and a study.'

'Where are the servants?'

'There are none at this time. A man and his wife from Vésinet wait upon Raoul. They come in the morning and go home after dinner.'

M. Verduret rubbed his hands with glee as he said:

'It will be a funny thing if we can't overhear some of the conversation between Raoul and the person who has come from Paris.'

They tried the door, but found it securely fastened, and then tried the ground-floor windows, also without success. M. Verduret was exasperated and walked around the house seeking an entrance and not finding one.

'Oh, if I could only see!' he cried.

Prosper was more surprised than ever at his companion's conduct, for the latter seemed quite at home in this garden into which he had climbed, and quite used to that kind of thing.

Suddenly a thought occurred to Prosper. 'There is a ladder,' he cried, 'at the bottom of the garden under the trees.'

They found the ladder with some difficulty, and raised it to the window, only to find it six feet short. M. Verduret overcame this difficulty by resting the bottom rung of the ladder upon his shoulders and told Prosper to ascend it.

Hardly had Prosper reached the window when he uttered a loud cry and fell to the ground. M. Verduret quickly put the ladder on the ground and ran to him saying:

'What is the matter?'

By that time Prosper was on his feet, and he answered in a harsh voice:

'Madeleine is there alone with Raoul.'

M. Verduret was surprised. He had expected to find a woman with M. de Lagors, but he thought that woman would be Madame Fauvel.

'Are you sure you are not mistaken?' he asked.

'Quite,' Prosper replied. 'But the thought that Madeleine, the noble and pure Madeleine, is the mistress of this man who was my best friend, is a horrible one. But I have been humiliated enough and will not be coward enough to bow my head to an insult like this.'

Prosper rushed towards the house, till M. Verduret stopped him and asked him what he meant to do.

'Take my revenge,' he replied. 'I will break down the door, enter the house and demand satisfaction.'

'You shall not do that, Prosper,' M. Verduret replied. 'If you make a noise Raoul will be put upon his guard, and escape, and you will remain dishonoured.'

'What does it matter?'

'It matters to me, for I have sworn to prove your innocence. You shall have your vengeance, but it is madness to kill a man when you can send him to prison.'

'What must I do then?'

'Wait. Vengeance is a delicious fruit which must be allowed to ripen.

'Besides,' continued M. Verduret, 'how do we know that Mademoiselle Madeleine is here on her own behalf? Are we not convinced that she is sacrificing herself?'

Prosper thought a moment and then said:

'Promise, sir, to tell me the whole truth, however painful it may be to me.'

'I give you my word of honour I will.'

Prosper raised the ladder and placed it upon his shoulders, saying as he did so, 'Go up.'

In a second, without a jerk upon the ladder, M. Verduret was looking in the window. He noticed that Madeleine had on her outdoor dress, her hat and cloak. She was standing in the middle of the room, talking animatedly, though displaying indignation and contempt.

Raoul was sitting on a low chair, stirring the fire with the tongs, and occasionally shrugging his shoulders, as if he had resigned himself to hear all that Madeleine had to say.

M. Verduret could not hear a word of what they were saying owing to the noise of the wind. It was evident to him that they were quarrelling, though it was not a lovers' quarrel. He watched Raoul's face, which was lit up by the lamp, and saw him now and then shudder in spite of his apparent indifference.

In despair Madeleine was imploring him with clasped hands and bowed head. She was almost on her knees.

He turned his head away and only answered her in monosyllables.

Two or three times Madeleine seemed about to go, but she returned as if to make one more effort. At last Raoul got up and handed her a packet of papers.

'Ah,' thought M. Verduret, 'compromising letters, I suppose!'

Madeleine did not seem to be satisfied. She continued to speak as if she were asking for something else; and on Raoul refusing she threw the papers down on the table.

The papers interested M. Verduret. They were pawn-tickets of various colours. Madeleine looked through the papers on the table, selected three, folded them and put them in her pocket. She was now determined to go, and Raoul took the lamp to light her.

M. Verduret descended the ladder carefully, and then he and Prosper laid it down out of sight and took up their positions in the shadow to watch.

Raoul and Madeleine appeared upon the doorstep, and the watchers could see him offer her his hand, which she refused with a scornful gesture. This repulse did not seem to surprise Raoul, who simply said:

'As you will.'

Madeleine got into the carriage, which went away at a rapid pace.

Prosper at once reminded M. Verduret of his promise to tell him the whole truth, and the latter replied:

'In less than a month you will regret that you suspected Madeleine of being Raoul's mistress. But we must go at once.

We cannot efface our tracks, but the tracks and the ladder will be put down to thieves.'

They climbed the wall and had hardly gone fifty yards along the road when they heard a gate shut and saw a figure going towards the station.

'It is Raoul,' said M. Verduret. 'Joseph will tell us that he has gone to tell Clameran of the scene. If they would only talk French—'

After a moment's silence he resumed: 'How came a gay young fellow like Lagors to live in a lonely house at Vésinet?'

'Because,' Prosper replied, 'M. Fauvel has a house a quarter of an hour's walk away on the banks of the Seine.'

'That explains the summer; but what of the winter?'

'In the winter he has apartments at the *Hôtel du Louvre*.'

They found the carriage which had brought them still outside the inn where they had left it an hour before and the driver inside. They explained to him, to account for their muddy condition, that they had got lost and got into a morass in the forest, and asked him to drive them back.

The drive back seemed very long to Prosper as he sat in silence, for he was chilled to the marrow. M. Verduret would not talk and seemed to be asleep. As a fact he was very annoyed. This expedition, which he thought would have swept away his doubts, had merely complicated them. The facts still remained, but the circumstances were changed.

The clock struck twelve as the carriage reached the *Hôtel du Grand-Archange*, and Madame Alexandré prepared supper for them in a few minutes. During supper Prosper noticed with what admiration she looked at his companion.

After supper M. Verduret got up and said to Prosper:

'You will not see me tomorrow during the day, but I shall be here about this time. I may find what I am looking for at the Jandidier's ball.'

Prosper was surprised at the idea of M. Verduret going to a ball given by the most wealthy financier in Paris, and said:

'Have you an invitation then?'

'Not yet,' he replied, 'but I shall have one.'

Prosper thought how fortunate he would be to see Madeleine, looking more beautiful than ever in her Maid of Honour's dress.

CHAPTER XI

THE mansions of the Jandidiers, the two celebrated financiers, are about the middle of the Rue Saint Lazare. They are side by side and quite distinct, though when necessary, as for special functions, they can be thrown into one. When the movable partitions are removed the reception-rooms are the finest in Paris.

The princely hospitality shown on these occasions made their functions the most popular and select.

The fancy-dress ball was on Saturday, and the costumes were of great richness and originality.

One of the most noticeable costumes was that of a clown who took up a position near the door. About half-past ten M. and Madame Fauvel and Madeleine entered.

M. Fauvel's dress consisted simply of a short silken cloak, but Madame Fauvel wore a magnificent court dress of the latter years of Louis XIV. She had been a remarkably handsome woman; and her magnificent costume made her look much younger than forty-eight, which was her age.

All eyes were fixed upon Madeleine, who looked like a queen in her Maid of Honour's dress.

It was a most magnificent spectacle which seemed to impress the clown as he stood by a window watching Madeleine dancing with a golden Doge who was none other than the Marquis de Clameran. The Marquis seemed to be paying court to her, and she was listening to him, if not with pleasure, at least without anger.

An old gentleman, wearing a Venetian cloak, stopped in front of the clown and said:

'You remember your promise, M. Verduret?'

The clown bowed respectfully and replied:

'Yes, you have my promise, Count.'

'Thank you; I know its value.'

During his short conversation with the Count the dance had ended and the clown had lost sight of M. de Clameran and Madeleine. He went in search of them and found Madeleine with Madame Fauvel and Raoul de Lagors in a long gallery which had been transformed for the night into a fairy garden.

Madeleine now seemed sad, and Raoul and Madame Fauvel were carrying on a serious conversation. In one of the card-rooms the Doge, M. de Clameran, had taken up a position from which he could see Madame Fauvel and Madeleine without being seen.

'Ah,' the clown thought, 'it is a continuation of yesterday's scene. These two fellows have the two women in their clutches, but how?'

A grand minuet had commenced in the ballroom, and the gallery was almost empty, when the clown decided that the right moment for his scheme had arrived.

He took up a position between the couch occupied by Madame Fauvel and the door of the ball-room, and began waving his banner, tapping with his wand and coughing affectedly like a man about to speak. The guests remaining in the gallery gathered round him, and he began to speak in the finest buffoon manner:

'Ladies and gentlemen . . . This morning I obtained permission to submit to you a spectacle which has met with some success. It is the translation of a drama which was first performed in Pekin. Take your places, ladies and gentlemen, please; the lights are up and the actors ready.'

The clown's idea was first of all to attract the attention of Madame Fauvel, whom Raoul and Madeleine had left sitting alone. In this he succeeded.

'Ladies and gentlemen,' the clown continued, 'we are in China. The first of the scenes represents the celebrated

Mandarin Le Fo in the bosom of his family. The beautiful young woman leaning on his shoulder is his wife, the most virtuous of women, who adores her husband and children. Being virtuous she is happy, for Confucius says "Virtue is more pleasant than vice".'

Madame Fauvel had gradually approached the group and taken a seat quite near the clown.

The clown after imitating the rolling of a drum continued.

'Scene II! The old lady sitting before the glass plucking out her grey hairs is the beautiful woman of the first scene. She is no longer beautiful, virtuous or happy. It is a very sad story. One day, in a street in Pekin, she met a beautiful young Bandit, and she loves him!'

While he was saying this the clown had partly turned, and was now facing the banker's wife.

'You are surprised, ladies and gentlemen,' he went on, 'but I am not. Bilboquet, my master, has told us that the heart never grows old. The poor wretch is fifty and she loves a youth. What a lesson this scene is! But there are times when the light of reason penetrates her skull, and the manifestations of her anguish would move the most pitiless. She understands the inanity, the folly and the ridiculousness of her passion. She admits to herself that she is pursuing a phantom, she knows only too well that the man who is radiant with youth cannot love her now she is old and only retains the remnants of her beauty.'

The clown kept his eyes fixed upon the banker's wife, but nothing he had said seemed to touch her. He began to wonder if he were upon the wrong track. He noticed, too, that M. de Clameran had joined his circle of listeners.

'In scene III,' he went on, 'the old woman, the Mandarin's wife, has got rid of her remorse. She has made up her mind that, as he does not love her, she must attract this handsome young fellow to her by his own interests. With this idea she presents him to the principal men of the city, and so that he may cut a good figure she gives him all her jewels. He takes them to the pawnbroker's, but refuses to give up the tickets to her.'

The clown was satisfied, for Madame Fauvel began to show signs of uneasiness. Once she made an effort to get up and go away, but she remained chained to her seat, forced to listen.

'But, ladies and gentlemen, there came a day when the Mandarin's wife had nothing more to give him. Then the young Bandit conceived the idea of stealing the Mandarin's jasper button, a jewel of incalculable value and the insignia of his dignity, which was kept in a granite strong room and guarded by three soldiers. The Mandarin's wife resisted for a long time, for she knew that the soldiers would be accused of the robbery and crucified, and the thought troubled her. But the man spoke in such tender tones that the jewel was stolen. The fourth scene represents the criminals stealthily descending the staircase.'

He stopped. Three or four of his audience had noticed that Madame Fauvel was taken ill and had gone to her assistance.

He felt his arm grasped, and turned to find M. de Clameran and Raoul de Lagors, pale and threatening, facing him.

'What do you desire, gentlemen?' he asked in his most courteous tones.

'To speak to you,' they answered.

He followed them across the gallery to a window which opened upon the balcony, where they were out of sight of everyone but the gentleman with the Venetian cloak whom the clown had addressed as 'Count'.

M. de Clameran was the first to speak.

'What is this abominable story you are detailing?'

'Abominable? If you care to call it so! I wrote it myself.'

'Enough, sir, enough; have the courage of your actions and admit that it is an insinuation against Madame Fauvel.'

The clown, with his head thrown back as if he were seeking ideas from the ceiling, listened with a bewildered air, though a malicious twinkle might have been observed in his eye.

'You have discovered,' the clown at last said, 'in the drama of the Mandarin's wife an illusion to Madame Fauvel whom I do not know from Eve. It is impossible!'

'Do you mean to say you have not heard of M. Fauvel's misfortune?'

'Misfortune?'

'I mean the robbery of which he was a victim.'

'Ah, yes, I know. His cashier decamped with 350,000 francs. But that is an almost daily occurrence, and what is there in my story like that?'

M. de Clameran hesitated before answering, for a hard dig from Lagor's elbow had calmed him. He looked at the clown suspiciously and seemed to bitterly regret his significant words.

'Well,' he said in a haughty tone, 'perhaps I am mistaken. After your explanation, I admit my mistake.'

'I have given you no explanation,' said the clown, taking up a defiant attitude.

'Sir.'

'Allow me to finish, if you please. If I have unwittingly wounded the wife of a man I esteem, he, it seems to me, is the judge of his own honour and the person to tell me about it. You will say that he is too old to demand satisfaction, but I have seen his son here. Who are you to constitute yourself Madame Fauvel's champion? Are you a relative of hers? What right have you to insult her by pretending to discover an allusion in what is only a story invented to please?'

Having no reply to make to this firm and logical remonstrance, M. de Clameran tried another tack.

'I am M. Fauvel's friend,' he said, 'and that title gives me the right to be jealous of his honour; and another reason, I shall soon be a member of his family. In a week my engagement to Mademoiselle Madeleine will be officially announced.'

This information took the clown quite by surprise, but he recovered himself in a second and said in a slightly ironical tone:

'Accept my congratulations, sir. Besides being Queen of the Ball, she has, it is said, a dowry of half a million francs.'

Raoul de Lagors had listened to this conversation with visible impatience, but Clameran went on:

'We cannot have an explanation with a man who conceals his identity.'

'You are quite at liberty to ask the master of the house who I am.'

'You are,' cried Clameran, 'you are—'

A gesture from Raoul arrested an insulting epithet, and after waiting a moment for the end of the sentence the clown said:

'I am, sir, your brother Gaston's best friend. In his lifetime I was his adviser and confidant.'

These simple words struck Clameran like a thunderbolt. He turned pale and recoiled as if he could see a spectre. He wanted to speak, but his words were frozen in his throat with fear.

'Come along,' said Lagors, who had retained his self-possession, and he dragged his friend away staggering like a drunken man.

The clown was almost as surprised at the effect of the words as the ironmaster had been at the words.

'What terrible memory,' he murmured, 'have I awakened in this wretch's soul?'

A tap on the shoulder from the gentleman with the Venetian cloak aroused him from his reverie.

'Are you satisfied, M. Verduret?' he asked.

'Yes and no, Count. No, because I have not completely attained my object in coming here. Yes, because the two rascals have committed themselves so much that doubt is no longer possible. I thank Providence for revealing a secret to me I did not suspect.'

The conversation was interrupted by the approach of five or six of the company, and the Count bade the clown a friendly adieu.

The clown at once went in search of Madame Fauvel, whom he found in animated conversation with Madeleine, and then he noticed Lagors and Clameran questioning various people.

'Ah,' he thought, 'they are trying to find out who I am.'

They soon gave up their quest, and after wishing Madame Fauvel and her niece good-night left the ball, followed shortly afterwards by the clown, a large overcoat concealing his costume.

Lighting a cigar, the clown was strolling towards the Faubourg Montmartre when a man rushed from the shadow and struck at him with all his strength. An instinct of self-preservation caused the clown to try and parry the blows, and this movement saved his life, for he received the dagger thrust in his arm.

Seeing that the blow had failed, the assassin did not renew the attack, but fled.

'I am sure it was Lagors,' said the clown, 'and Clameran is not far away.'

The wound, though not dangerous, was a severe one and very painful, but the clown bandaged it with his handkerchief with the dexterity of a surgeon.

'I must be on the track of something very serious,' he thought, 'for them to attempt murder.'

After satisfying himself that his arm was not quite useless, he went after his assailant, taking care to keep in the middle of the road. He could see no one, but he was certain he was being watched.

When he reached the Boulevard Montmartre, as he crossed the road he recognized two shadows which crossed a little higher up.

As he walked along the Boulevard, still followed by his enemies, M. Verduret turned over in his mind the situation. He was sure that they wanted to find out who he was now, not to assassinate him, and if they succeeded they would fly at once.

He could have them arrested, but by acting precipitately he might perhaps assure the safety of the principal criminal, M. de Clameran; for there was no conclusive evidence against him.

After careful consideration, the clown decided to act alone till he had enough evidence to convict the guilty.

The next thing to do was to give the men who were following him the slip. He walked at a good pace till he came to the Square des Arts et Métiers. Here he stopped short and spoke to two policemen, asking them some unimportant question.

This manoeuvre resulted in Raoul and Clameran stopping twenty yards away. While he was talking to the policemen the clown had rung the bell of the house in front of which they were standing and had heard the door open. He wished the policemen good-night and entered the house quickly.

A minute or two later, after the policemen had gone, Raoul and Clameran rung the bell too, and made the porter get up to ask him who the individual was who had just entered in a clown's dress.

The porter was unable to tell them who it was, but they learned from him that the house had another entrance in the Rue Saint-Denis.

'We are done,' said Lagors; 'we shall never find out now.'

M. Verduret reached the *Hôtel du Grand-Archange* at three o'clock and found Prosper impatiently waiting for him. The first thing that M. Verduret did was to bathe his wound, which was very painful.

'That is a souvenir of your friend Raoul,' he said to Prosper as he showed it to him.

'Now,' he continued, 'let us talk. Our enemies are warned; we must strike like lightning. I was mistaken. I was on the wrong track. I mistook the effect for the cause, I must admit. The day on which I believed I had discovered that guilty relations existed between Raoul and Madame Fauvel, I considered that I held the end of the thread which led to the truth.'

'Is she innocent then?'

'No, certainly not, but she is not guilty in the way we supposed. I thought that she was enamoured of this good-looking young adventurer, and had given him her family name, and introduced him to her husband as her nephew, to open the door of her house to adultery. She began by giving him all her money; then she gave him her jewels to pawn; and then, having nothing else, she allowed him to rob her husband's safe. That was what I thought.'

'In that way everything is explained,' said Prosper.

'No; I knew that did not explain everything, and that is where I made my mistake. How does that theory explain Clameran's influence?'

'He is merely Lagor's accomplice.'

'That is the mistake. I believed, too, that Raoul was the chief criminal, but he is not. Yesterday, in an argument between them, the ironmaster said to his old friend: "Do not resist me, or I will break you like a piece of glass." Lagors is not Madame Fauvel's creature, but Clameran's damned soul. Madeleine, too, is in the power of Clameran, not Lagors.'

Prosper tried to protest. M. Verduret could have convinced him by telling him that Clameran had announced to him his approaching marriage to Madeleine; but he refrained from doing so, wishing to spare the young man's feelings, and being sure that he would be in time to prevent the wedding.

'Clameran alone,' continued M. Verduret, 'has Madame Fauvel in his power. What is this mysterious power he has over her? Madame Fauvel has always been above suspicion, and it is only fifteen months since they met again for the first time since their childhood. So it is to the past we must look for the secret of this domination.'

'We know nothing,' Prosper murmured. 'We shall discover everything when we inquire into Clameran's past. When I mentioned his brother Gaston's name tonight he turned pale and recoiled as if he saw a ghost. I have often thought that Gaston's death, when his brother was visiting him, was very sudden.'

'Do you suspect murder?'

'I can believe anything of people who try to assassinate me. Now the robbery has become a mere detail. It is easy of explanation. I know who secured the key and who obtained the word.'

Prosper got up with his eyes shining with hope.

'Perhaps the key was M. Fauvel's?' he said.

'You were the person who betrayed the word. You have forgotten, no doubt, but fortunately your mistress has a good memory. Do you recollect having supper with Madame Gypsy, Lagors and two other friends two days before the robbery? Towards the end of the supper she quarrelled with you.'

'Yes, I remember that.'

'Do you know what answer you made her?'

'No.'

'Ah! Well, you said to Nina: "You are wrong to reproach me with not thinking of you, for it is your name which secures my employer's safe".'

Prosper made a wild gesture.

'Yes,' he cried, 'I remember.'

'Then you know the rest. One of the two forced Madame Fauvel to give him her husband's key. She only obeyed after terrible threats had been used. She was very ill on the morning after the robbery, and she it was who sent you the 10,000 francs.'

'Who was the thief, Raoul or Clameran? What hold have they over Madame Fauvel? And how is Madeleine mixed up in the affair?'

'I cannot answer those questions, Prosper, yet. That is the reason I don't wish to have them arrested. Give me another ten days, and if by that time I have not found out these things, I will tell M. Patrigent what we know. In an hour I shall be on the road to Beaucaire, which is the neighbourhood from which Clameran and Madame Fauvel come.'

'Yes, I know their families.'

'Neither Raoul nor Clameran shall escape, for the police will keep them under observation. But while I am away, Prosper, you must swear to remain a prisoner here.'

Prosper took the required oath, but could not help asking M. Verduret the reason he was giving him his powerful aid.

'I will tell you,' the latter replied, 'before Nina the day you marry Madeleine.'

Left to himself, Prosper considered the extent of the investigations of his mysterious protector, and was obliged to admit that he himself would have been quite powerless without his aid.

Twice, during his enforced confinement at the *Grand-Archange*, where he never even looked out of the window, he had news of M. Verduret. The first time he received a letter from him stating he had seen his father who had given him assistance. The second time Dubois, M. de Clameran's valet, came on behalf of him whom he called his chief to say that everything was progressing favourably.

On the ninth day of Prosper's seclusion he decided against Madame Alexandré's advice to take a walk late in the evening. He entered a café to quench his thirst, and picking up a paper saw the announcement of the approaching marriage between the niece of the famous banker, M. André Fauvel and the Marquis Louis de Clameran.

Prosper, mad with sorrow, lost his head and made up his mind that it was necessary to create an obstacle to the marriage in case M. Verduret was too late. He called for pen and paper, and disguising his writing as much as possible he wrote to his old master:

'DEAR SIR,

'You gave your cashier up to justice as you were sure of his infidelity.

'But if he stole your money, did he steal your wife's diamonds and pawn them?

'If I were you I would watch my wife, and you will find that it is necessary to distrust second cousins.

'Also before signing Mademoiselle Madeleine's marriage contract, I would inquire at the Prefecture of Police about the noble Marquis de Clameran.

'A FRIEND.'

Prosper made haste to post his letter, though after he had done so it occurred to him that he might be upsetting all M. Verduret's plans.

On his return to the hotel Prosper found that Joseph Dubois had been to tell him that M. Verduret had completed his inquiries and would be back at nine o'clock the following evening.

M. Verduret had succeeded, with the help of information from several old servants of Clameran and Lagors, the inhabitants of Vésinet, and notes from the Prefecture of Police, in reconstructing the following drama of the past.

CHAPTER XII

THE DRAMA

THE château of the Clamerans stood on the left bank of the Rhône. It was black with age and neglected, but still strong.

In 1841 the old Marquis de Clameran and his two sons, Gaston and Louis, lived there.

The old Marquis was a member of the old aristocracy, who seem as if their clocks stopped in 1789, and who have the manners of another century.

He looked upon events since '89 as a series of deplorable pleasantries and ridiculous efforts on the part of the mob. He had returned from exile in 1815 and found a part of his immense domains still able to provide him with an honourable existence.

His income was about 15,000 francs a year, but his expenditure was about 25,000 or 30,000 francs, for he lived in hopes of a real restoration which would give him back the whole of his immense domains.

His two sons followed his example. Louis spent his time in search of amusement and adventure, while Gaston sought to initiate himself in the life of the period by reading and work.

The old Marquis in his egoistic heedlessness was the happiest of mortals. He was beloved by his peasantry and hated by the poor of the neighbouring towns. His principal distraction was to slander his neighbour and *bête noire* the Countess de la Verberie.

The Countess was a tall gaunt woman, haughty and contemptuous, who, like the Marquis, had returned from exile in 1815.

Unlike her neighbour, her income was only 2,500 francs a year, the Château de la Verberie and its small domain being all she could obtain from her protectors and the royal munificence.

The Château de la Verberie, though not so large as its neighbour, was of reasonable size and convenient, and was built in the middle of a most beautiful park extending from the road to Beaucaire to the river.

Here the Countess lived, cursing her life, with her only daughter, Valentine, a beautiful blonde girl of sixteen, the fame of whose beauty had spread far and wide.

The Countess execrated M. de Clameran as much as he detested her. Their hatred was broader and deeper than the river which flowed between the two châteaux. Its origin was difficult to state with exactness. The story ran that in the reign of Henry IV or Louis XIII, a La Verberie had seduced a Clameran. A duel had followed; there had been swords gleaming in the sunlight and blood on the grass. The facts were not very clear, but that was the story.

Gaston had seen Valentine at a fête and fallen in love with her. She had seen him, too, and could not help thinking of him.

They did not see one another again for nearly a year, till they both of them spent an entire day with the old Duchess d'Arlange. This time they spoke and seemed like old friends.

After this it was months before they spoke again, though they used to see one another across the river at certain times. But one evening in the month of May, when Madame de la Verberie was at Beaucaire, Gaston ventured into the park and met Valentine, who was neither surprised nor angry.

They walked together without talking of love, for they seemed to recognize the hopelessness of it, and made up their minds to only meet once more.

The next interview, however, was not the last. As the distance to the nearest bridge was a league, and Gaston did not wish to make use of a boat, he learned to swim across the river. Then they met every evening.

They believed that the secret of their meetings was not known, but they had been watched. One November night, when the river was too high and the current too strong to make swimming possible, Gaston had gone to Tarascon to cross by the bridge. He dined at an hotel there with a friend, and after dinner, while playing billiards, overheard the conversation of five young fellows who were playing dominoes. Gaston turned as white as a sheet, and going up to the table where the five were sitting addressed the eldest, Jules Lazet, by name.

'Repeat,' he said in a voice trembling with anger, 'what you have just said.'

'Why not?' Lazet calmly replied. 'I said that girls of noble birth are no more virtuous than work girls.'

'You mentioned a name.'

'I mentioned,' he said, 'the name of the pretty little fairy of La Verberie.'

The remainder of the people in the hotel had gathered round them, and from the remarks and faces of the crowd Gaston perceived that he was surrounded by enemies.

'Only a miserable coward,' he went on, 'would insult and calumniate a young girl whose mother is a widow, and who has neither father nor brother to defend her honour.'

'But she has her lovers,' Lazet replied with a sneer.

These words were too much for Gaston. He raised his arm and struck Lazet on the cheek.

There was a scene of wild confusion as Lazet jumped over the table and seized Gaston by the throat, for his herculean strength and violent temper were well known. Gaston's friend tried to assist him, but he was surrounded, knocked down with billiard cues, and pushed under the table.

Lazet, who was a brave fellow, called out to the others to leave them alone; but the others were too excited to do so. Five or six of them rushed at Gaston, who picked up a knife from one of the tables and struck twice at the person nearest to him.

It was Jules Lazet. He fell to the ground, and the others rushed at Gaston, armed with anything they could get, to take his life. Finding escape impossible, after receiving several wounds, Gaston jumped on to the billiard table, and from there sprang through the front window of the café into the street.

Gaston de Clameran, though he was cut and bleeding in twenty places, set off in the direction of his home, pursued by the crowd. A gate barred his path. He tried to burst through it, but fell back seriously hurt, and was at once surrounded by his pursuers, who shouted, 'To the Rhône with the Marquis.'

Unfortunately he still had the knife in his hand, and mad with fear he struck down two more.

Once more he escaped, and this time distancing his pursuers reached the château in safety. He at once sought out his father, told him the story, and asked for the means to leave the country. His father gave him all the money he had, 920 francs, and the jewels which had belonged to his mother.

Before departing Gaston told his father that the quarrel had arisen over Valentine de la Verberie, whom he loved, who was his mistress, and whom he wished to marry. His desire to marry her aroused his father's anger, and as they were engaged in a fierce dispute the servants rushed in to say that the gendarmes were coming.

Gaston's escape was now cut off. His only chance was to attract the attention of his pursuers in one direction while he endeavoured to escape in another. It was arranged that two horsemen should ride out of different gates to attract the pursuers while Gaston endeavoured to escape over the park wall to the river.

The plan would probably have been successful had not one of the horses ridden by his brother Louis stumbled and fallen before it had gone far. The pursuers soon found out that they were pursuing the wrong man and returned to the château in time to see in the moonlight Gaston climbing the wall.

'There is our man,' said the officer in command.

Gaston's route lay across an immense field of madder, which it was impossible for the horses to cross in the dark, so he did not despair.

He reached the river in safety and took up his position, pistol in hand, on the end of an uprooted tree trunk which was lying half in the water.

The officer in charge of the gendarmes called upon him to surrender. The noise of the river drowned his voice so that the fugitive could not hear him.

Throwing his pistols from him, Gaston dived head first into the river. The shock loosened the tree, which turned over and drifted down stream.

The gendarmes seemed grieved at the death of this fine young fellow, whom they had pursued with such vigour. They admired his courage, energy, and his resignation, for being armed he could have sold his life dearly.

CHAPTER XIII

THAT evening Valentine was on the bank of the river awaiting her lover. She noticed lights flitting about the Château de Clameran opposite in quite an unusual way, and had a presentiment of evil. She had never seen the river so wild and swift.

When Gaston rose to the surface after his plunge, he did not waste his strength trying to stem the current, but allowed himself to drift with it. Before he had gone far he saw the tree trunk from which he had dived floating swiftly down the stream, and after a severe struggle managed to reach it.

A little below the park of La Verberie the river makes a sharp bend, and here Gaston reckoned on being able to land. But it was some distance lower down before the tree trunk was near enough to the bank to make a landing possible.

As soon as Gaston reached the bank he set off in the direction of La Verberie at top speed. He got there none too soon, for Valentine was almost mad with anxiety and grief.

He soothed her and then told her that the secret of their love had been discovered; he gave an account of the struggle, which had ended in him becoming a fugitive from justice, and begged her to fly with him.

She refused to go, being unwilling to leave her mother in poverty as she was and without a friend.

Gaston was stupefied at her unexpected decision, and it seemed to him that another Valentine had risen before him; but he made up his mind to obey her.

'You order me to go without you,' he cried, 'and I will obey you. In three years I shall have made my fortune or be dead. But before continuing my flight I have a sacred trust to give you.'

Taking from his pocket the silk purse with the jewels in it, just as his father had given it to him, he went on:

'These are my mother's jewels, and you alone are fit to wear them. If I do not return in three years to claim them, you will know that I am dead, and then you will keep them in remembrance of him who loved you so dearly.'

She hesitated and tried to refuse, but he insisted, and then said:

'Now, I have a last request to make! Everyone thinks that I am dead, and that will be my safety. But I cannot leave my old father in despair. Swear to me that you yourself will go and tell him that I am safe.'

'I will go, I swear it,' she replied; 'but where are you going?'

'To Marseilles, where I can get a friend to conceal me and obtain a passage for me to a foreign country.'

'You cannot go like this. I will find you a guide and companion in whom you can have the utmost confidence, our neighbour Menoul, the owner of a boat on the Rhône.

They left the park and went to the old sailor's house, where he was sitting by the fire. He was very surprised to see them together and got up rubbing his eyes, thinking he was dreaming.

'Menoul,' Valentine said, 'the Count is obliged to conceal himself, and desires to reach the sea and get on board ship secretly. You will be rendering me a great service if you will take him down to the mouth of the river in your boat.'

The old man shook his head doubtfully, and then replied:

'For your sake, mademoiselle, I will do so; though at night, with the river in its present state, it is no easy job.'

The old man found Gaston dry clothes and Valentine watched them board the boat, after embracing Gaston for the last time.

Three days later, thanks to Menoul, Gaston was concealed in the hold of the American three-master, *Tom Jones*, Captain Warth, sailing the next morning for Valparaiso.

CHAPTER XIV

STANDING motionless on the river bank Valentine watched the boat bearing her lover drift down with the current. Although Gaston had retained a ray of hope, she herself had none.

She returned to the château sobbing and overwhelmed with despair, and reached her own room without being noticed. Here she examined the jewels Gaston had entrusted to her, and after kissing them in memory of her absent lover, concealed them.

At daybreak the following morning she dressed and set off to fulfil her promise, leaving a message for her mother that she had gone to Mass. Her difficulty was to return by breakfast-time, for the distance she had to go, owing to the bridge over the river being so far away, was five leagues.

Valentine set off at her best pace, but it was eight o'clock before she reached the avenue leading to the château. Here she met Saint Jean, the Marquis' valet, whom she knew well. His eyes were red with weeping and his face was agitated. He did not raise his hat to her as usual, but asked her roughly if she were going to the château. She replied that she was. The servant said that if she were going to see M. Gaston, it was useless, as he had died for his mistress.

Valentine turned pale at the insult, but went on:

'I want to speak to Monsieur the Marquis.'

Saint Jean sobbed, and then said:

'You need go no further, for he died at five o'clock this morning. When the news was brought to him of his son's death, it was just as if he were struck by lightning. He beat the air with his hands and fell back without a cry. He regained consciousness for a few moments about daybreak and desired to be left alone with his son Louis. His last words were:

"Father and son on the same day, there will be rejoicing at La Verberie".'

When Valentine heard that the old Marquis was dead she was obliged to lean against a tree for support; she could have calmed the old servant's grief, but was afraid she might be committing a fatal indiscretion by telling him that Gaston was alive.

'Ah, well, then,' she said, 'I must speak to Monsieur Louis.'

This declaration seemed to astound Saint Jean.

'Would you have the audacity,' he cried, 'after what has happened? Be advised by me and return home, for I will not answer for the servant's tongues if they see you.'

Without waiting for a reply he walked rapidly away.

There was nothing for Valentine to do after her humiliation but to return home. On her way she met one of the servants, who told her that her mother had received a visit in the morning and since then had been calling for her and was in a frightful state of mind.

An old dowager, a friend of the Countess, had given her an exaggerated account of the scenes of the previous evening, and the ruin of her daughter's prospects of marriage rather than her loss of reputation had enraged her.

When Valentine saw her mother, there was a fearful scene, which ended by her falling at her mother's feet in a faint and being carried to her room. On recovering consciousness she appeared to be seriously ill and her mother was persuaded to call in a doctor.

After his examination the doctor pronounced Valentine to be seriously ill and also enceinte.

Her mother determined as soon as Valentine was well enough to take her away, and for this purpose disposed of half her securities for 25,000 francs.

At last they started, taking with them Mihonne the servant, after making her swear upon the Bible to keep the object of the journey an eternal secret.

The Countess, her daughter and servant went to reside in a small village near London, in the name of Madam Wilson. The Countess had selected England as their residence, because she had lived there for a long time and knew the language and the ways of the people. She had still friends among the aristocracy, and often dined in town and went to the theatre afterwards, leaving Valentine at home locked in her room.

In this solitary house, Valentine de la Verberie gave birth to a son, who was christened by the clergyman of the parish, Valentin Raoul Wilson.

In the village the Countess had discovered a farmer's wife who, for the sum of £100, had agreed to adopt the child and bring him up as her own. To her he was handed a few hours after birth.

This woman did not know the Countess' real name and thought she was an Englishwoman, so it was more than likely that when the child grew up he would not discover the secret of his birth.

When Valentine recovered her senses and asked for her child her mother was pitiless.

'Your child is safe,' she replied, 'and will lack nothing. Let that suffice for you; you must forget what has happened like a bad dream. Let the past be as if it never existed. You know me; that is my wish.'

Valentine had the thought of resisting her mother's despotism, but she had not the courage to do so. She kept silence and submitted to her mother's will.

Towards the end of June, Valentine was well enough to return to La Verberie. The secret of the voyage had been well kept and the doctor was the only person who was aware of its real object. The Countess, though she hated him, was sure that she need not fear an indiscretion on his part.

The loss of part of the Countess' small income was a serious matter to her, and a ceaseless subject of complaint against her daughter, for she could not make ends meet. To make up the deficiency, the Countess started borrowing, and in four years she had sold the rest of her securities and owed 40,000 francs, on which she could not even pay the interest.

During this time nothing had been heard of Gaston, who, as there was no proof of his death, had been sentenced by default to several years' imprisonment. As for his brother Louis, it was not exactly known what had become of him, though some said he was leading a gay life in Paris.

About this time a young engineer, André Fauvel by name, who was engaged in work connected with the Rhône, had made the village near La Verberie his centre of operations.

He had noticed Valentine, watched her, and made up his mind even before speaking to her to make her his wife. He was fairly rich and had a brilliant career before him.

He mentioned his hopes to an old friend of Madame de la Verberie and learned her embarrassed financial position. This raised his hopes, though he had no friend to whom he could entrust the task of asking for the lady's hand. Luck, however, was his friend.

One evening he entered the hotel at Beaucaire to dine and saw Madame de la Verberie about to take her place at table. He asked her permission to be allowed to sit near her, and she gave it with a smile.

The Countess, who had come to Beaucaire to negotiate a loan and had not been successful, began to complain of the hard times, and perhaps it was her anger at her lack of success which made her confide in this young man, whom she hardly knew, more than in her most intimate friends. She told him her position, her anxiety for the future and the sorrow she felt at being unable to marry her dear daughter.

This was the young engineer's opportunity. He sympathized with her and said that he knew more than one man who would feel it an honour for Mademoiselle Valentine, even without a dowry, to take his name, and consider it a duty to see that his mother-in-law was free from financial worries.

Besides a sufficient sum to pay off her debts, 60,000 francs, could be arranged as a loan. Then, too, no man loving Valentine would leave her mother without a regular income. This, of course, for the sake of appearances, need not be included in the marriage contract, but could be treated as the interest on a sum of money which had been received.

Although nothing definite had been said between the Countess and the young engineer as to who the son-in-law was to be, they thoroughly understood one another, and when the Countess wished him good-night, she invited him to dinner the following day.

Madame de la Verberie had not been so joyful for years, for the prospect seemed quite brilliant when compared with her present desperate straits. But an idea occurred to her which made her turn cold with horror.

'Would Valentine consent?'

So great was her anxiety that she at once, on her return home, went up to her daughter's room and said:

'A young man, who seems to me a very suitable match, has asked me for your hand, and I have given my consent.'

The suddenness of this statement paralysed Valentine.

'It is impossible,' she stammered. 'Have you told him the truth, mother?'

'God forbid that I should mention your past folly,' her mother replied; 'and you will do well to keep silent too.'

'Would you have me, mother, commit the most cowardly and infamous treachery by marrying a man without confessing the truth to him?'

The Countess had great difficulty in restraining her anger, but she well enough knew how futile her threats would be against this conscientious resistance. She pleaded:

'Poor child,' she said, 'poor, dear Valentine, if you only knew our horrible position, you would not say that. Your folly was the beginning of our ruin, now we have reached the climax. Our creditors are threatening to turn us out of La Verberie. What will become of us then? Must I, at my age, start begging from door to door? We are ruined, and this marriage is our only hope of salvation.'

The Countess used many other arguments, and Valentine, who did not know what to do, begged for a few hours to think it over. These her mother could not refuse her.

After a sleepless night, Valentine rose in the morning with her mind almost made up to speak, but when in the evening she was sitting near André Fauvel, with her mother's threatening and imploring eye upon her, she decided to put off telling him the truth till another day.

For a long time Gaston had remained like a dazzling hero in Valentine's mind, but time had gradually dimmed her idol's brilliance, and it was now only a cold relic. This, combined with the Countess' attitude, which betokened misery in every way, as if she were already starving, persuaded her to accept the attentions of this young engineer, whom, she could see, loved her dearly.

Valentine did not yet love him, but his presence was pleasant and a separation would have been cruel and sad to her.

The Countess was quite as impatient as André for the wedding to take place and pressed on the preparations. She gave Valentine no time to reflect, but kept her occupied with a thousand details.

At last one evening she was alone with her lover for the first time. Her anguish was more bitter than usual and she burst into tears. André noticed her tears and begged her to confide in him. She was on the point of telling him the truth, but the thought of the scandal, André's grief and her mother's anger, stopped her. She made up her mind that it was too late.

The following day the marriage of André Fauvel and Valentine de la Verberie took place in the village church.

Her husband adored her. He had gone into business and been successful, but he was anxious to become very wealthy to surround his beloved wife with every luxury.

Eighteen months after her marriage Madame Fauvel gave birth to a son. But neither this son nor the one she had a year later could make her forget her other child which had been adopted by a stranger.

Though she loved her sons passionately and brought them up like little princes, she often said to herself:

'Perhaps the outcast has nothing to eat!' Sometimes, too, she said to herself:

'Misfortune has forgotten me.'

But misfortune is a visitor who sometimes keeps people waiting, but always comes at last.

CHAPTER XV

LOUIS DE CLAMERAN, the second son of the Marquis, had one of those cold and nonchalant exteriors, which concealed in his case a fiery temperament and furious passions. All kinds of extravagant thoughts were in his head long before the events which decided the destinies of the house of Clameran.

Though apparently taken up with futile pleasure, this precocious hypocrite in reality was bored by his existence in the country and the small towns in the neighbourhood, and was thirsting for independence, wealth, fame and pleasure.

He did not love his father and hated his brother like poison. The old Marquis himself had sowed the seeds of this hatred by his oft repeated declaration that at his death he would leave everything he possessed to his elder son, and Gaston's assurance that the estate should be divided between them had not touched Louis' heart.

The servants were aware of this hatred, which the Marquis and Gaston had never even suspected, and a scene took place between Louis and Saint Jean, whose fifty years' faithful service had gained him a freedom which he sometimes abused.

'It is very unfortunate,' said the old servant, 'that such a skilful horseman as you are should have fallen just at the moment when your brother's safety depended upon your riding. The other horseman did not fall.'

The young man turned pale at this terrible insinuation and said:

'Rascal, what do you mean?'

'You know well enough, sir,' Saint Jean had insisted.

'No, speak, explain yourself!'

The servant's only reply was a look, which was so signifi-cant that Louis rushed at him with his riding-whip raised and would have struck him but for the interference of the other servants.

This scene had taken place while Gaston was trying to escape from his pursuers, and a few minutes later the gendarmes and hussars returned with the news that he had dived into the Rhône and had most assuredly perished.

Louis remained quite unmoved when the news was brought, but there was a gleam of triumph in his eye and he had no hesitation in telling his father the news, and in a firm voice said:

'My brother has chosen between life and honour . . . he is dead.'

At these words the old Marquis had tottered and fallen like an oak struck by lightning. Towards the morning Louis watched his father breathe his last without a tear.

Louis was master now, for the measures taken by the Marquis to elude the law and ensure his eldest son taking the whole of his property on the day following his death without dispute defeated his object.

By the culpable assistance of his solicitors and a fraudulent conveyance this had been effected, and now Louis was the recipient even without the production of his brother's death certificate.

Louis was Marquis de Clameran now with a fortune of 200,000 francs. His sudden acquisition of wealth turned his head, for it was noticed that he followed his father to the grave with his head bowed, a handkerchief to his mouth and a smile on his face.

The new Marquis' first action was to sell everything and discharge all the servants, and within a week he had left the château, taking an oath, as he did so, never to return to it, and taken the coach to Paris.

The young Marquis felt sure that when he was in Paris, his land of promise, the city of his dreams and ambitions, he would be, with the help of his title and fortune, a person of importance.

He had made a great mistake, for there was nothing in him to constitute a personality; he was lost in the crowd, a drop of water in the midst of a torrent.

The only privilege his title gave him was to open the gates of the Faubourg Saint Germain to him and make him acquainted there with men of his own age and rank, whose income was equal to a half or the whole of his capital. Almost all these young nobles confessed that they had to limit their vices, follies and extravagances, but this did not open his eyes. He learned to imitate them in their extravagances.

If he had no friends he had a number of acquaintances, who introduced him into smart society, and in three months he had attained a reputation as a good fellow and had been gloriously compromised by a smart girl.

He took comfortable rooms, with a coach-house and stabling for three horses, near the Madeleine, and when he had furnished the rooms with necessaries he found that his three months in Paris had cost him 50,000 francs, a quarter of his capital.

The Marquis soon ran through the remainder of his capital, and after living for a time upon the fame of the fortune he had spent and the credit that remained, one day his creditors fell upon him in a body and he had to let them have the remnant of his wealth, his furniture, horses and carriages.

He moved to more modest rooms, though he could not break with the rich young men whom he believed to be his friends. He borrowed where he could and never repaid. He gambled, and when he lost did not pay. He became an adventurer and made use of the experience he had bought at the cost of 200,000 francs.

He became mixed up in a blackmailing and card-sharping affair without actually having committed a criminal offence, but an old friend of his family, the Comte de Commarin, came to his rescue and provided the means for him to cross to England.

In London the Marquis descended to the lowest rung of the ladder of vice and lived in a world of swindlers and prostitutes, whose profits he shared. When he was compelled to leave London he traversed the whole of Europe without any other capital than his audacity, corruption and skill as a card-sharper.

At last, in 1865, after eighteen years' absence from France, he had a stroke of luck at Hamburg and returned to Paris, thinking he had been forgotten.

His first thought was for the country of his birth, not that he had any friends or relatives there, but before his departure his solicitor had been unable to find a purchaser for the château, and perhaps by this time a purchaser had been found.

Three days later, one beautiful October evening, he arrived at Tarascon, and after making sure that the château was still his property, he set out to walk to Clameran.

On reaching the village he went to the house of his old servant, Saint Jean, only to learn from the latter's son that his father had been dead five years.

On learning that he was the Marquis de Clameran, the son, whose name was Joseph, welcomed him with open arms and introduced his wife Antoinette, a good-looking dark young woman with big black eyes.

In a few minutes they had prepared a meal for the Marquis. The news of his return soon spread through the village, and the peasants came to pay their respects to him.

After a time the Marquis summoned up courage to ask for the keys of the château. Here he found a state of ruin and desolation, both within and without. All the furniture which Louis had not dared to sell was still there, but it was nothing but a few pieces of wood and a few shreds of cloth.

After a good look round the Marquis said:

'The château will soon be as bad as the furniture if something is not done. My fortune does not permit of my restoring it, so I must try and find a purchaser for it while it is still standing.'

This idea seemed like sacrilege to Joseph, but he had not the courage to say so.

'Would it be difficult,' Louis went on, 'to sell this tumble-down house?'

'It all depends upon the price, sir. I know a man in the neighbourhood who would buy it at a bargain.'

'Who is that?'

'A man named Fougeroux, who lives on the other side of the Rhône at Montagnette. He is a Beaucaire man who twelve years ago married a servant of the late Countess de la Verberie named Mihonne.'

'When can I see him?' the Marquis asked.

'Today if you like.'

As they were crossing the river in the ferry boat, on their way to see Fougeroux, Joseph warned the Marquis against his ruses.

'He is an old fox,' he said. 'When Mihonne married him she was fifty, and he was only twenty-five. He married her for her money, and now he ill-treats her. Now he has introduced another woman into the house and Mihonne has become her servant. He is a wonderful man at making money, and is rich today, but he owes it all to her.'

They went to a fine well-cultivated farm and asked for M. Fougeroux. A little man with a red beard and an uneasy and furtive eye soon appeared.

Although he affected to despise the aristocracy and the priesthood, the prospect of a good deal reduced M. Fougeroux to a state of abject servility.

He invited them in at once, and turning to an old woman who was sitting in the chimney corner ordered her brutally to go and get a bottle of wine for the Marquis de Clameran.

This name acted like an electric shock upon the old woman, who seemed to have something to say which a look from the tyrant stopped. She obeyed his order and took her seat again, staring at the Marquis with open mouth.

Could this be the fat jolly Mihonne who was the maid of the little fairy of La Verberie? Even Valentine would not have recognized her after her years of misery.

The deal took place between Joseph and Fougeroux, and after a lot of bargaining the latter agreed to give 5,280 francs for the château and the land, leaving the remains of the furniture to Joseph.

While Fougeroux was gone to look for a bottle of his best wine to seal the bargain, Mihonne took the opportunity to address the Marquis.

'I must see you alone, sir,' she said. 'I have a secret of life or death to tell you. Will you meet me at nightfall under the walnuts over there?'

Just then her husband returned with the wine and they filled their glasses again.

On the way back Louis did not know what to make of this singular rendezvous.

'What can the old woman want with me?' he asked Joseph.

'Who can tell?' he replied. 'She was in the service of the woman who was M. Gaston's mistress, my father told me. If I were in your place I should go after dinner.'

About seven o'clock Louis reached the spot the old woman had pointed out to him, and found her there. Her first words were to ask him if he had heard anything of his brother.

'You know very well,' Louis replied, 'that my brother jumped into the Rhône and was drowned.'

'What!' Mihonne cried. 'Don't you know he was saved? He swam across the river. The next morning Mademoiselle Valentine went to Clameran to let you know, but Saint Jean prevented her from seeing you. When I took a letter for you afterwards, you had gone away.'

These revelations staggered Louis.

'Are you sure you are not dreaming?' he said gently.

'Quite,' she replied, 'and if Menoul were alive he would tell you how your brother embarked at Marseilles. But besides that M. Gaston had a son by Mademoiselle Valentine, and I bore this poor innocent to the woman who adopted him.'

Then she told him the whole story of the journey to London, the birth of the child, Valentine's misery, and her marriage to a rich Paris banker, Fauvel by name.

She was interrupted by a loud shout, and went back to the farm as fast as her legs could carry her. Her husband was calling her.

Louis stood still for a minute after she had gone, for an infamous idea had occurred to him and was gradually shaping itself.

He knew the rich banker by reputation, and thought that if this story, on verification, turned out to be true, it would be worth a lot of money to him.

That was the reason which led him to start for London the next day after receiving the 5,280 francs from Fougeroux.

CHAPTER XVI

THOUGH married more than twenty years Valentine de la Verberie, Madame Fauvel, had only suffered one sorrow, the death of her mother, in 1859, from inflammation of the lungs while on one of her frequent visits to Paris.

Her husband was the same to her now as he had been when they were married. He was richer than he had ever even hoped to be. Their two sons, Lucien and Abel, were a credit to the family, and Valentine had adopted an accomplished young girl, Madeleine, an orphan niece of M. Fauvel's, and loved her as her own daughter.

The day of the orphan's arrival M. Fauvel had opened a banking account with 10,000 francs for her as a dowry. Though not a daring speculator on his own behalf, the rich banker had amused himself by speculating with this money in the most risky securities, and in fifteen years the 10,000 francs had become 500,000 francs.

In this atmosphere of happiness Valentine had almost forgotten the past and her conscience was nearly at rest, for she had suffered so much that she believed she had expiated her offence. She believed she was quite safe.

One November afternoon, during her husband's absence in the country, she received this letter, which had been left by a man who refused his name:

'MADAME:
    'Am I counting too much upon a memory of your heart to hope for half an hour's interview?
    'I shall do myself the honour of calling upon you between two and three o'clock tomorrow.'
                                        'MARQUIS DE CLAMERAN.'

Happily Madame Fauvel was alone, for a frightful feeling of anguish overtook her. Then she began to reassure herself by thinking that it must be Gaston who had written the letter and wished to see her once more. But terrible doubts still assailed her. Should she tell Gaston that she had had a son by him? If she did so she put herself entirely at his mercy. If she kept silent she was committing a crime.

But even at half-past two the following afternoon, when the Marquis de Clameran was announced, she had not made up her mind what to do.

A man of about fifty, with hair and moustache turning grey, a sad and severe expression, and an air of distinction, was shown in and remained standing in the middle of the room.

Madame Fauvel gazed at him, looking for some likeness in him to the man she used to love so dearly, and finding none. At last she murmured:

'Gaston!'

He shook his head sadly and replied:

'No, madame, I am not Gaston. My brother died in exile; I am Louis de Clameran.'

A shudder of fear traversed her at the thought that this was not Gaston. What could he want, this brother in whom, she knew, Gaston had not enough confidence to let him know their secret?

She overcame her fears so quickly that Louis hardly noticed them, and with a nonchalant gesture offered him a seat, saying as she did so:

'Be good enough, sir, to explain the object of your visit.'

Keeping his eyes steadily fixed upon Madame Fauvel, the Marquis sat down.

'First of all, madame,' he said, 'I must ask you whether we are likely to be overheard?'

'Why that question? I do not think you have anything to tell me which my husband and children cannot hear.'

'Allow me to insist on your own account,' he said with a shrug of the shoulders.

'Speak, sir, without fear; we are quite private here.'

The Marquis drew his seat close to Madame Fauvel's, so that he might talk to her in a low voice.

'I told you, madame,' he began, 'of my brother's death. He confided to me his last thoughts and wishes. I will not recall to your memory the fatal events which ruined my brother's life and future. Happy though your life has been, you cannot have forgotten the friend of your youth, who gave his life when your honour was endangered?

Madame Fauvel did not move a muscle of her face; she appeared to be trying to recall the circumstances to which Louis was alluding.

'Have you forgotten, madame?' he went on in a bitter tone. 'It was long ago that you loved my unfortunate brother. It is useless to deny it, madame; Gaston told me everything.'

Madame Fauvel saw no reason to be frightened at this, for Gaston had gone away without knowing that she was enceinte, so assuming an assurance she did not feel:

'You seem to forget, sir,' she said, 'that you are speaking to an old married woman, the mother of a family. Your brother may have loved me, but that is his secret, not yours. If in my youth I was not quite as prudent as I ought to have been, it is not your place to remind me of it. He would not have done so. The past you are recalling I have forgotten for twenty years.'

'Even your child, madame?'

Madame Fauvel was thunderstruck, and the thought which occurred to her was: 'How could he have found out?' But in defence of her own and her family's happiness she displayed quite unexpected energy.

'You are insulting me, sir!' she said.

'Then you do not recollect Valentine Raoul?'

'Are you doing this for a wager?' Madame Fauvel could see that this man knew everything. But her mind was made up to deny it all, even in the face of the most obvious proof. She thought of having the Marquis turned out, but prudence stopped her.

'Two years ago,' the Marquis went on, 'my brother Gaston was in London. He met a young man named Raoul, whose face and intelligence so impressed him that he tried to find out who he was. He was an adopted child, and after inquiries my brother was certain that Raoul was his son, and yours, madame!'

'This is a romance you are telling me.'

'Yes, madame, a romance, and the sequel is in your own hands. The Countess, your mother, took the most minute precautions to preserve your secret, but after your departure one of her London friends came to the village and mentioned her real name to the farmer's wife who had adopted the child. My brother obtained the most positive proof of this.'

He stopped to watch Madame Fauvel's expression, but to his great surprise she gave no sign of anxiety. She smiled and said lightly:

'What then?'

'Gaston recognized the child. But the Clamerans are poor; my brother died in a lodging-house, and my income is only 1,200 francs. The thought of what would become of Raoul without friends and relatives tortured my brother's last hours.'

'Really, sir.'

'Then it was that Gaston opened his heart to me. He ordered me to come to you. "Valentine," he said to me, "will remember; she will not be able to bear the thought that our son is without everything, even bread; she is very rich, so I die happy."'

Madame Fauvel had got up obviously to end the interview.

'You admit, do you not, sir, that my patience is very great?'

Her calm assurance dumbfounded Louis, who made her no answer.

'I am willing to tell you,' she went on, 'that I was in M. Gaston de Clameran's confidence. As a proof of it I am going to return to you your mother's jewels, which were entrusted to my charge by your brother on his departure.'

She handed him the purse containing the jewels, saying as she did so:

'Here they are, sir. I am surprised that your brother never came himself to claim them.'

Louis displayed surprise at this, but said in a dry tone:

'My orders were not to speak of this trust.'

Madame Fauvel rang the bell to have him shown out; and he did not think it was policy to insist on remaining.

'Very well, madame,' he said, 'I will retire. I can only add that my brother said: "If Valentine has forgotten and refuses to provide for her son's future, I command you to force her to do so." I swore to do so, madame, and I will keep my word.'

As soon as Madame Fauvel was alone she shut herself up in her own room and gave way to despair. What were her twenty years' happiness compared with this hour of despair?

She gave up all hope. This man, who left her with a threat, would return, and then what reply could she make him?

When she came to think over this story which Louis had told her, there seemed to be gaps and improbabilities in it. Why had Gaston lived in poverty in Paris without asking her for the jewels he had entrusted to her charge? Why had he not come to see her about the child's future, as he was anxious about it and knew she was rich?

One moment she thought of telling her husband the whole story, but she gave up the idea when she thought of the sorrow he would feel. He might doubt her fidelity as a wife when he discovered her girlish indiscretion.

She knew her husband well enough to be certain that he would stifle the scandal, but the happiness of the household would be ruined.

Then she thought of suicide; but her death would not stop the implacable Clameran who would dishonour her memory.

Fortunately the banker was away, and Madame Fauvel was able to keep to her room for a couple of days and conceal her agitation.

Madeleine guessed that there was something more serious the matter than the nervous disorder for which the doctor prescribed, but could do nothing.

On reflection Madame Fauvel decided to give way. She knew she was undertaking an impossible life; but she was the only one to suffer, and there was a chance of salvation.

M. Fauvel returned home and his wife resumed, in appearance at least, her ordinary life. She expected every moment to hear from Clameran. Every time the door opened she turned pale, and she dare not go out lest he called in her absence.

At last a letter came, in which he pleaded illness as an excuse for making an appointment for the following day at the *Hôtel du Louvre*.

She burned the letter and made up her mind to go.

Dressing herself as plainly as possible, she walked some distance before engaging a carriage to take her to the *Hôtel du Louvre*, for being well known she was afraid of being seen entering the hotel.

At last she summoned up courage to enter the hotel and to knock at the Marquis de Clameran's room door on the third floor. A voice told her to enter, which she did and found herself confronted by a very young man, almost a child.

Madame Fauvel, thinking she had made a mistake, began:

'I beg your pardon, sir, I thought this was the Marquis de Clameran's room.'

'You are quite right, madame,' the young man replied. 'I believe I have the honour of addressing Madame Fauvel?'

She gave an affirmative nod with her head, for she was terrified at the thought that Clameran had already betrayed her secret.

'Be quite easy, madame,' the young man went on, 'you are as safe here as in your own house. M. de Clameran has asked me to present his apologies to you, for you will not see him.'

'But, sir, after his urgent letter I thought—'

'When he wrote to you, madame, he had plans which he has now abandoned.'

Madame Fauvel was too surprised and troubled to reflect, and the young man's face had an expression of sad compassion upon it.

'The Marquis,' he said in a sad and gentle voice, 'has given up what he wrongly thought to be a sacred duty. After his interview with you, blinded by anger, he swore to obtain by fear what your heart withheld. Determined to wreck your happiness he collected all the evidence against you.'

He took a bundle of papers from the mantelpiece and went on:

'These proofs are indisputable. They consist of the Reverend Sedley's certificate, a statement by Mrs Dobbin the farmer's wife, a doctor's certificate, and the depositions of people who knew Madame de la Verberie in London. I had considerable difficulty in obtaining them from M. de Clameran, and this is what I mean to do with them.'

He threw the papers on the fire and watched them reduced to ashes.

'They are all destroyed,' he went on. 'The past is blotted out, the proofs are destroyed, and you are free.'

At last Madame Fauvel began to understand. This young man who had delivered her from Clameran's anger was the adopted child, Valentin Raoul. In a moment her mother's feeling, so long suppressed, overcame her, and in a hardly audible voice she said, 'Raoul!'

The young man trembled and seemed to bend beneath the weight of his unexpected happiness.

'Yes, I am Raoul,' he cried, 'and I would rather die a thousand times than cause my mother any suffering.'

She opened her arms and Raoul rushed into them saying in a choking voice:

'Mother, mother, thank you for this first kiss.'

Madame Fauvel had sunk down on a couch and was gazing in ecstasy at Raoul, who was kneeling at her feet.

How beautiful this love-child seemed with his fine wavy hair, his pure white forehead, his fine eyes and red lips.

'Mother,' he said, 'you do not know what my feelings were when my uncle dared to threaten you. When his brother told him to go to you he was no longer in his right senses. Often my father and I lingered near your house, and when we had seen you we were happy.'

Madame Fauvel was weeping, for this voice recalled Gaston's to her, and the time between Gaston's last embrace and the present seemed to have passed away.

Raoul went on:

'I did not find out till yesterday that my uncle had been to you to beg on my behalf. Why should he? It is true that I am very poor, but misery does not terrify me, and I have strength and intelligence to support myself. You are very rich, mother, I am told; but keep the whole of your fortune and give me a little of your heart. Promise me that this first kiss shall not be the last. No one shall find out anything, for I can conceal my happiness.'

How Madame Fauvel reproached herself with being afraid of this son! She asked him about his life.

The farmer's wife who adopted him had always displayed some affection for him and given him an education beyond his station. At sixteen he obtained employment at a bank, and had begun to earn his living when his father came and took him away. Since then he had lacked nothing but a mother's love. The only time he had suffered was the day his father, Gaston de Clameran, had died in his arms.

Suddenly Madame Fauvel realized that it was seven o'clock, and that perhaps her long absence would be noticed; she got up to go.

'Shall I see you again, mother?' Raoul asked.

'Yes,' she replied tenderly, 'often, every day, tomorrow.'

For the first time since her marriage Madame Fauvel perceived that she was not mistress of her actions; for never before had she so desired uncontrolled liberty as she did now. Her feelings towards her husband and sons seemed to have entirely changed. She seemed no longer to be a loving wife and incomparable mother. Her soul seemed to be in the little room of the *Hôtel du Louvre*.

It was half-past seven before Madame Fauvel reached home, and found that dinner was waiting. M. Fauvel joked about her lateness, but she knew that neither he nor her sons would suspect the thoughts which agitated her mind; yet she was afraid of her niece.

On her return Madame Fauvel thought that Madeleine looked at her curiously. Did she suspect anything? During the last few days, too, she had asked her many curious questions. She must be distrustful of her. But to her great joy she discovered a way to get rid of her uneasy solicitude and devotion.

For nearly two years there had been thoughts of a marriage between Madeleine and Prosper Bertomy, M. Fauvel's cashier and protégé, and Madame Fauvel made up her mind to expedite matters as much as possible. When Madeleine was married she would live with her husband, and that would leave her days at her own disposal.

The same evening Madame Fauvel gave Madeleine to understand that both M. Fauvel and herself were in favour of her marrying Prosper, and said to herself:

'I will get André to encourage Prosper, and in less than two months they can be married.'

Madame Fauvel spent part of each day with Raoul at the *Hôtel du Louvre* and was greatly exercised in her mind as to how she could make a position for him and give him an independent fortune. Her only fear was that he would decline to accept anything from her. The Marquis Louis de

Clameran, whom she had frequently seen since the day he had frightened her, and whom she loved for the affection he displayed to her son, came to her rescue.

One day the Marquis broached the subject:

'To live the life he is living,' he began, 'is, no doubt, very charming for my nephew; only would it not be wise for him to think of making a position for himself in the world? He has no fortune—'

'Dear uncle,' Raoul interrupted, 'let me be happy without remorse; what do I lack?'

'Nothing just now, my fine nephew; but when you have exhausted my resources and your own—which will not be very long now—what will become of you?'

'I will enlist, for all the Clamerans are soldiers by birth.'

Madame Fauvel put her hand gently over his mouth, saying reproachfully:

'Naughty boy! Would you deprive me of the pleasure of seeing you?'

'No, dear mother, no.'

'You must listen to us,' Louis insisted.

'I will do so later on. I will work and become rich.'

It was difficult to make this presumptuous young man listen to reason, and very hard to choose a profession for him. Clameran thought that it was necessary to reflect and to consult the young man's tastes. While doing so, it was arranged that Madame Fauvel should provide for Raoul's expenses.

Seeing in Gaston's brother a father for her child, Madame Fauvel soon found him indispensable to her, and was glad when he suggested that she should receive him openly at her own house.

She introduced the Marquis de Clameran to her husband as an old friend of her family, and he soon became a constant visitor; for as she dare not see Raoul every day, nor receive his letters, she obtained news of him through his uncle.

In less than a month after Madame Fauvel had found her son, the Marquis de Clameran told her that Raoul was a source of considerable uneasiness to him. He had the pride and passions of the Clamerans and was capable of all kinds of folly. He had done nothing irreparable yet; but it was his future which alarmed his uncle.

Madame Fauvel made the usual excuses for her son.

'Perhaps you are a little severe,' she said. 'Happiness may have turned his head. He has been so unfortunate.'

'You are quite right,' the Marquis said; 'it is excusable. He does not yet know of your goodness to him. He thinks he is spending my money and is as extravagant as a millionaire's son. Will you not, madame, talk seriously to him and try to obtain employment for him?'

Madame Fauvel promised, but did not keep her promise, for her interviews with Raoul were so short that it seemed a great pity to spend the time in chiding him.

The Marquis suggested that it would be for Raoul's benefit if she could see him every day.

'Alas,' the poor woman replied, 'that would be my dearest wish. But what am I to do? I have my duty to my other sons.

This reply seemed to surprise the Marquis, for she had not spoken of her family before.

'I will think it over,' Louis said, 'and perhaps at our next interview I shall be able to suggest a plan.'

The reflections of a man of such experience could not be in vain, and he appeared quite pleased when he called on the following Thursday.

'I have sought and found it,' he began.

'What?'

'The means of saving Raoul.'

He explained that the only way for Madame Fauvel to see Raoul every day without arousing her husband's suspicion was to receive him at her own house.

'Impossible!' she cried.

'Yes,' the Marquis replied thoughtfully, 'but it would be the boy's salvation.'

She resisted with an energy which would have discouraged a less firm will than that of the Marquis de Clameran, but at the end of a week she had begun to discuss the means of executing the plan.

'How?' she said. 'Under what pretext can I receive Raoul?'

'Have you not at Saint Rémy an aged relative, a widow with two daughters?'

'Yes; my cousin, Madame de Lagors.'

'Is she well off?'

'No; she is very poor.'

'Yes, and without your secret assistance she would have to depend on charity.'

'Do you know that?' Madame Fauvel said, surprised at the Marquis being so well informed.

'Yes, madame; I know that and many other things too. I know, for instance, that your husband does not know any of your family; is not even aware of the existence of your cousin. Do you understand my plan now?'

She half-understood it now and was trying to find a way of opposing it.

'This is what I propose,' Louis went on. 'Tomorrow, or the day after, you will receive a letter from your cousin at Saint Rémy, saying she is sending her son to Paris and asking you to look after him. Naturally you will show the letter to your husband, who a few days later will give Raoul de Lagors a hearty welcome.'

'My cousin,' Madame Fauvel cried, 'is an honourable woman and will never lend herself to this revolting comedy.'

The Marquis smiled a conceited smile.

'Did I say,' he asked, 'that I should take your cousin into my confidence? The letter you receive will be dictated by me to a woman and posted at Saint Rémy by a trustworthy person. Do you see any obstacle now?'

'My will,' she cried, 'of course does not count. It is a crime, an abominable crime.'

Clameran got up, and his evil passions gave his pale face an atrocious expression.

'I think,' he went on, 'we misunderstand one another. Before talking about crime, let us remember the past. You were less fearful when as a young girl you took a lover, though you did refuse to follow him when he fled the country. You had not these prejudices when, after a clandestine accouchement, you abandoned your child and absolutely forgot him, not caring, though you were worth millions, whether he had bread to eat or not. Where were your scruples when you married M. Fauvel? Did you tell this honourable man the truth? It is too late. You have lost the father, madame, but you shall save the son, or, upon my honour, you shall no longer steal the world's esteem.'

'I will obey,' she murmured, entirely crushed.

Eight days later Raoul, who had become Raoul de Lagors, dined at the banker's between Madame Fauvel and Madeleine.

CHAPTER XVII

MADAME FAUVEL had tried every possible way to escape from submitting to the will of the pitiless Marquis de Clameran. In despair, she turned to her son for assistance.

Raoul, as he listened to her, seemed transported with indignation, and had hastened, so he said, to make the wretch, who had caused his mother to weep, apologize.

He returned sadly with bent head and features contracted by impotent rage, and declared that she must give way.

The poor woman began to realize the depth of the abyss into which she had fallen, and the far-reaching results of the fault or imprudence she had committed by making that appointment with Gaston long ago. Since that time she had struggled in vain against the implacable logic of events, she passed her life in a struggle against the past, and now it had crushed her.

What a punishment it was to her to introduce Raoul to her family! The banker received him with a smile and the remark 'that Paris is better than Saint Rémy when a man is young and rich'.

Raoul took pains to make himself worthy of the cordial reception he had received. In less than a week he had worked his way into M. Fauvel's good graces, had conciliated Abel and Lucien, and had quite captivated Prosper Bertomy, M. Fauvel's cashier, who spent his evenings with the family.

Since Raoul had been introduced into wealthy society, he had become very extravagant and led a very dissipated life. After a short time his demands on his mother for money became incessant. At first she had given gladly, but she soon perceived that if her generosity were not limited it would be her ruin.

Ever since her marriage Madame Fauvel had taken what money she pleased for her own private use and the household expenses. But as she had always been so modest in her tastes and administered her household so carefully, she could not suddenly start spending large sums of money without comment. By chance the banker might discover the astonishing increase in the household expenses.

In three months Raoul had spent a small fortune. If Madame Fauvel remonstrated with him, his eyes filled with tears and he said:

'I am a child, a poor fool. I forget I am the son of the poor Valentine and not of the rich Madame Fauvel.'

He was also jealous of Abel and Lucien.

'They are happy,' he said, 'for they entered life by the golden door. They have friends and the consideration of the world.'

'But what do you lack, naughty boy?' Madame Fauvel asked in despair

'Nothing in appearance, but everything in reality. I have no right to your caresses, the comforts I enjoy, nor the name I bear.'

Madame Fauvel did anything to prevent him envying her two sons.

In the spring Madame Fauvel suggested that Raoul should take up his residence in the country, near her estates at Saint Germain. He was agreeable and took a place at Vésinet.

After Raoul had been to the races and lost 2,000 francs, M. Fauvel told him that when he was short of money he would lend him some. At the end of the week he borrowed 10,000 francs from the banker.

For some time the Marquis de Clameran had almost ceased to visit Madame Fauvel, so she decided to write to him and ask him to call and see her, in the hope that he might be able to do something to restrain Raoul's extravagance.

When the Marquis learned what had happened, he seemed even more annoyed than Madame Fauvel and a terrible scene took place between him and Raoul.

But Madame Fauvel became suspicious, for it seemed to her that their anger was a pretence, and that while they quarrelled there was laughter in their eyes.

She dare say nothing, but this doubt intensified the punishment she was enduring, though it was the Marquis she accused in her mind of abusing the weakness and inexperience of his nephew.

She tried to imagine the Marquis' object in this conduct, but he soon enlightened her. One day after complaining more bitterly than ever of Raoul's conduct, the Marquis said that he could only see one way of preventing a catastrophe; that was for him, the Marquis de Clameran, to marry Madeleine.

The Marquis' unexpected declaration cut Madame Fauvel to the quick, for though she had renounced all hope of happiness herself, by so doing she had hoped to preserve that of her family.

'Do you think, sir,' she cried, 'that I will lend my aid to your odious conspiracy?'

'Would it then be, madame, such a great misfortune for Mademoiselle Madeleine to become Marquise de Clameran?'

'My niece, sir, has chosen her husband. She loves M. Prosper Bertomy.'

The Marquis shrugged his shoulders disdainfully.

'A girl's fancy,' he said; 'she will forget him, if you wish her to. But we are wasting time. Be good enough to give way.'

'No, I will not,' Madame Fauvel replied firmly.

'I look upon the marriage as most important,' he went on, taking no notice of her refusal, 'to put matters straight. The money you provide Raoul with is not sufficient for his extravagance. There will come a time when you will have no more to give him and will be unable to conceal your expenditure from your husband. Madeleine's dowry will enable me to make up the deficit and save you.'

'I would rather be ruined than saved by such means.'

'But I will not allow you, madame, to compromise us all. We are associated in a common object: Raoul's future.'

'Cease to insist,' she said. 'I have quite made up my mind. Rather than submit to your shameful tyranny any longer, I will tell M. Fauvel the truth. He loves me and will forgive me.'

'You think so?' Clameran said with a sneer. 'You think that a man of M. Fauvel's excellent character will forgive your audacity and duplicity? What do you think he will say when he finds out that your pretended nephew, who sits at his table and borrows his money, is the fruit of your first love? Ah, well, it will be a great consolation to you when your husband and sons desert you and the honour of the name you bear is sacrificed, to be able to say to yourself: "Prosper, the worthy cashier, is happy!"'

'Come what may,' Madame Fauvel replied, 'I will tell my husband.'

'You will do as I wish you!' Clameran cried. 'Your niece's dowry is indispensable to us, and I love her. Now, madame, weigh my reasons. Think of the honour of your house and not of your niece's love affairs. I will come in three days for your answer.'

The Marquis had delivered his blow and decided that it would be wise to await the effect. He resumed his habitual nonchalance, and bowed with ceremony as he went out.

Madame Fauvel's energy was not a pretence. She was determined to tell her husband.

Directly the Marquis had gone, Madame Fauvel heard a footstep, and looking round saw Madeleine, pale and cold as a statue, coming towards her.

'This man must be obeyed, aunt,' she murmured.

On each side of the drawing-room, separated from it only by tapestry, was a little card-room, and Madeleine had been in one of these rooms, without her aunt knowing it, and overheard the conversation with the Marquis de Clameran.

'What,' cried Madame Fauvel in terror, 'you know?'

'Everything, aunt.'

'You want me to sacrifice you?'

'I beg you on my knees to allow me to save you. I hate and despise M. de Clameran, and he will always be to me the most cowardly of men, but I will be his wife.'

Madame Fauvel was dumbfounded at the grandeur of her devotion.

'But what of Prosper, poor fellow, whom you love?'

'Tomorrow,' Madeleine replied with a sob, 'I shall have broken with him for ever.'

'No,' cried Madame Fauvel, 'it shall never be said that I allowed you to suffer for my faults.'

Madeleine shook her head sadly:

'It shall never be said,' she replied, 'that I allowed your house to be dishonoured when I could prevent it. I owe everything to you and my uncle, and when your happiness is threatened, why should I hesitate? I will be Marquise de Clameran.'

Madame Fauvel struggled against her niece's generosity and devotion, but her resistance became weaker.

'What would your life be with this man?' she said.

'He says he loves me,' Madeleine replied, trying to appear hopeful, 'perhaps I shall be happy. But I wish I could obtain a large sum of money, that is all he wants. There is a doubt, too, which torments me. Does M. de Clameran mean to help his nephew. After he has obtained my dowry, perhaps he will abandon you and him too.'

Madame Fauvel looked at her niece in surprise.

'Go on,' Madame Fauvel insisted, 'I can bear anything.'

Madeleine hesitated and then said:

'I should like to be sure that M. de Clameran and Raoul are not in collusion and playing parts they have learned.'

Madame Fauvel could not and would not believe in such an odious comedy.

'That is impossible,' she said; 'the Marquis is angry at his nephew's conduct, and would never give him bad advice. But Raoul is vain and extravagant, though he has a good heart. If you could only see him when I reproach him, all your suspicions would disappear. When he swears with tears in his eyes to be more reasonable, he does so in good faith. Bad company is the cause of his failure to keep his promises.'

'I hope to heaven what you say is true,' Madeleine murmured, 'then my marriage will not be in vain. We will write to M. de Clameran this evening.'

'Why this evening, Madeleine? There is no hurry.'

'We had better get it over, aunt, dear,' she said firmly. 'Do you know what those anxieties you have been trying to conceal have done? Have you looked at yourself in the glass during the last four months?'

Taking her aunt by the hand she led her to a mirror, saying, 'Look at yourself.'

Madame Fauvel was only a shadow of her former self. In four months she had grown old. Sorrow had made its mark upon her brow.

'Do you understand now the need for security?' Madeleine went on. 'Do you see what a miracle it is that uncle has not noticed the change in you? I guessed you had a secret, but I thought perhaps you loved a man other than uncle.'

Madame Fauvel groaned, for if Madeleine had suspected her, so might others.

'My honour is lost,' she murmured.

'No, aunt, dear,' the young girl cried, 'take courage. There will be two of us to struggle now.'

M. de Clameran was very pleased that evening when he received a letter from Madame Fauvel saying that she would consent to everything. She only asked for a little time.

The following day Madeleine took Prosper on one side and tore from him the fatal promise not to see her again and to take the responsibility of the rupture upon himself.

Directly Prosper had gone away heart-broken, the Marquis de Clameran came to tell Madame Fauvel that as soon as he had her word and that of her niece he would consent to wait, for he knew that M. Fauvel was not favourably disposed towards him, and that a time would soon come when a deficit impossible to account for would hasten the marriage.

Madame Fauvel took up her residence earlier than usual in the country, and Raoul had gone to live at Vésinet. The country, however, did not make him any more economical. He had gradually cast aside all hypocrisy, and now only came to see his mother when he wanted money, which was very often. The Marquis, on the other hand, kept out of the way as much as possible.

There was a big dinner three weeks later at the banker's, to which the Marquis had been invited. During dessert the banker suddenly turned to him:

'Have you any relatives of the same name?' he asked.

'Not that I know of, sir.'

'For a week I have known another Marquis de Clameran.'

The Marquis turned pale and appeared disconcerted.

'Oh!' he stammered, 'you suspect my right to the title?'

M. Fauvel was rather pleased at the opportunity to tease a guest whose title had often annoyed him.

'Marquis or not,' he resumed, 'the Clameran in question appears to be in a position to do honour to the title. He seems very wealthy, for I have been instructed by one of my clients to make a payment of 400,000 francs to him.'

Clameran had wonderful control over his face, but Madeleine and her aunt noticed his start of surprise, and caught the rapid glance he threw at Raoul.

'The new Marquis appears to be a business man,' he said.

'I am afraid I cannot tell you. All I know is that the money came from shippers at Havre after the sale of the cargo of a Brazilian vessel.'

'Has he just come from Brazil, then?'

'I do not know, but I can tell you his Christian name if you would like to know it.'

The banker took out a morocco case and, after looking at a notebook for a moment, said:

'Ah, here it is! His name is Gaston.'

Louis by this time had recovered his audacity and was prepared for anything.

'Gaston,' he said in an off-hand way, 'I have it. This gentleman must be the son of a sister of my father's whose husband lives in Havana. On his return to France he has probably taken his mother's name as it is more sonorous than his father's, which was, if I remember right, Moirot or Boirot.'

'You will probably meet him here at dinner before long,' the banker said. 'He is coming to Paris as, of the money I was instructed to collect for him, he left 300,000 francs with me for the present.'

'I shall be pleased to make his acquaintance.'

The effect of the name 'Gaston' had been very striking. Raoul, who was usually such a brilliant talker, was quite disconcerted and remained silent, watching his uncle. Madame Fauvel and her niece were very disturbed, and continued to exchange the most significant glances.

After dinner, when the guests had risen to go into the drawing-room, Clameran and Raoul managed to remain behind. They made no effort to conceal their anxiety.

'The game is up,' Raoul said, 'we had better be off.'

But Clameran was an audacious adventurer, and was not disposed to give up while there was a chance left. He uttered a joyful cry when he saw the banker's notebook lying on the sideboard.

'Keep watch,' he said to Raoul; 'now we can discover where this other Clameran is to be found.'

He turned over the pages quickly and found the entry.

'Gaston, Marquis de Clameran, Oloron, Basses-Pyrénées.'

'How does that help us?' Raoul said; 'and, besides, the two women suspect something.'

'Come, we must join the other guests or our absence will be noticed. Keep cool and look cheerful or your attitude will betray us.'

Madeleine, advancing on tiptoe, had seen Clameran consulting the banker's notebook, and that confirmed in her mind the infamy of the man she had promised to marry.

When two hours later Clameran went back to Vésinet with Raoul, he had made his plans. The question was whether Gaston knew that Fauvel was the husband of Valentine or not. If he knew it, there was nothing for it but flight. If he did not know it there was a chance. The only way to find out was to go and ask him, and this Clameran decided to do, leaving Raoul at Vésinet, and promising to let him know if there was any danger.

Clameran's last words to Raoul were:

'But during my absence turn over a new leaf, and become a good son. Calumniate me if you can, but do not be foolish, and do not ask for money.'

CHAPTER XVIII

GASTON, after leaving Valentine, had great difficulty in effecting his escape, and but for the devotion and experience of his guide Menoul, he would not have succeeded, for 920 francs was all the money he had.

While Gaston remained in hiding at a farm at Camargue, Menoul went to Marseilles and discovered an American three-master whose captain, M. Warth, would be pleased to shelter a young fellow who might be useful on the voyage.

'It will be hard work,' Menoul had told Gaston, 'and the crew and captain are a very rough lot.'

'I have no choice but to go,' Gaston replied.

Before he had been on board the *Tom Jones* forty-eight hours, Gaston discovered that he was among a remarkable collection of bandits of the worst kind. Fortunately his rough and unaccustomed duties took up all his attention, preventing reflection on his part, and when his rest time came he was so worn out by fatigue, that he slept.

Sometimes he thought of the oath he had taken to come back in three years with a fortune and wondered if he should be able to keep his oath, but when he looked around him, he did not seem to be far on the road to this desired fortune.

The *Tom Jones* had sailed for Valparaiso, but Captain Warth proposed to visit the Gulf of Guinea on the way, and Gaston discovered that the vessel was engaged in the slave trade. This discovery filled him with anger and shame, but he disguised his feelings, for he knew very well that his eloquence would have been wasted on the captain as the profits were so large.

The crew had a certain amount of respect for Gaston, for the story of his knife thrusts had leaked out, and when, after three months, the second officer died, he was chosen to take his place. In this capacity he made two voyages to the Gulf of Guinea and helped to carry a thousand negroes and land them secretly on the coasts of Brazil.

It was more than three years from the time he embarked at Marseilles before he could leave Captain Warth at Rio Janeiro, and when he did so he had 12,000 francs as the result of his voyages.

As soon as he landed in Brazil he wrote to one of his friends at Beaucaire for news of his home and friends, and also to his father.

The following year he received the reply and learned that his father was dead, his brother Louis had left the country, Valentine was married, and he himself had been sentenced to several years imprisonment.

This letter overwhelmed him. He was alone in the world now, without relations, dishonoured by a sentence of imprisonment, and deprived of his life's sole aim by the marriage of Valentine.

In his rage he said to himself, 'I will make money; that is the only thing which never deceives.'

He set to work. He speculated in skins, a mine, and farming. Five times he went to bed a rich man and woke in the morning ruined. At last, after long years of struggling, he acquired a million francs and a vast tract of land.

As soon as he became a wealthy man, the love of his native land came back to him, he wished to die in France. After making sure that there was no fear of his arrest on the old charge, he realized as much as he could of his property and embarked.

After an absence of twenty-three years and four months he landed at Bordeaux on a fine day in January, 1866. He had sailed a young man full of hope, but returned with white hair, believing in nothing.

The change of climate was too much for his health, and for several months he suffered with articular rheumatism.

The doctors ordered him to the South, and after he was completely cured he was so attracted by the beauty of the Valley of Aspe that he made up his mind to live there.

He realized that idleness would kill him, so he bought an iron foundry near Oloron on the banks of the Gave, with the object of utilizing the immense quantities of wood in the mountains, for which there was no means of transport.

He had been there a few weeks when the card of a gentleman who wished to see him was brought in.

It bore the name: Louis de Clameran.

For many years Gaston had not felt such emotion. The blood rushed to his head, and he trembled.

'My brother,' he cried, 'my brother!'

He hurried downstairs, and finding his brother waiting in the hall, clasped him in his arms and dragged him into the drawing-room. They sat down facing one another.

'It is you,' Gaston said in a loud voice. 'It is you! I should have recognized you anywhere. Your expression has not changed. You have the same look and the same smile.'

Louis was smiling, perhaps as he smiled on the night when the fall of his horse handed Gaston over to his captors. He appeared pleased and happy.

It had required all Louis' courage, will-power, and the feeling of necessity to come. His teeth chattered with fear as he gave his card to the servant. So great was his anxiety that when he saw his brother rushing down the stairs, he was tempted to flee. He had not said a word, standing as if petrified, but now that he was almost certain that no suspicion had ever crossed his brother's mind, he smiled.

'Now,' Gaston went on, 'I am no longer alone in the world. I shall have someone to love, and so me.'

He stopped, and then asked almost

'Are you married?'

'No.'

'So much the worse! I should like to have seen you the husband of a good woman and the father of fine children. But still I have a brother, a friend to whom I can talk.'

'Yes, Gaston, a good friend.'

'Ah, well, we will live our bachelors' lives together. You make me feel young again; I feel only about twenty now and as strong and vigorous as when I swam across the Rhône. But since then I have struggled, suffered, changed and grown old.'

'What?' Louis interrupted, 'you don't look as old as I do. I should have known you anywhere, you are just the same.'

Louis spoke the truth. He himself appeared worn out rather than old; but his brother, though his hair was grey and the Brazilian suns had burned his face a brick colour, was a robust man in the prime of life.

'But how did you find me?' Gaston asked.

In the eighteen hours he had spent in the train Louis had prepared his answers.

'We must thank Providence,' he replied, 'for our reunion. Three days ago I met a young man who told me he had spoken to a Marquis de Clameran here. I wondered what impostor had taken your name, so I took the train at once to find out.'

'Did you not think of me then?'

'Ah, brother, I thought you had been dead for twenty-three years.'

'Dead! Did not Mademoiselle de la Verberie let you know that I had escaped? She promised to go and tell my father.'

Louis assumed the broken-hearted expression of a man forced to disclose the truth.

'Alas,' he murmured, 'she told us nothing.'

A wave of anger passed over Gaston at the thought that Valentine had been pleased to get rid of him.

'What,' he cried, 'had she the barbarity to let you mourn me, to let my father die of grief? She must have been ly afraid of scandal; she sacrificed me for her reputation.'

did you not write?' Louis asked.

'I wrote as often as possible; it was from Lafourcade that I learned that father was dead and you had left the country.'

'I left Clameran because I thought you were dead.'

Gaston got up to try and shake off the sadness which had overcome him.

'But why worry over the past?' he said. 'The future is before us. I am a terrible gossip, and perhaps you have not yet dined.'

In half an hour the brothers were sitting down to a good dinner. Louis told his brother all that happened after his departure, and when he admitted he had sold the château, Gaston said:

'I should not have done so myself, but still remembrance is in the heart, not in a few old stones. I dared not go back to Provence, for I feared my sufferings in seeing Clameran and the park of La Verberie would be too acute.'

The fact that his brother had not been to Provence removed one of Louis' most serious doubts, and the following day he sent this telegram to Raoul:

'Be wise and prudent. Follow my instructions. All is well and I have great hopes.'

But though Gaston had been so open, his brother had not obtained the information he came to seek. He made up his mind to find this out at all costs, and breakfast was a favourable opportunity.

'Do you know, Gaston,' he began, 'that we have talked about everything but serious business?'

'Whatever is it you are looking so serious over?'

'Why, thinking you were dead, I took possession of our father's property.'

Gaston interrupted him with a hearty laugh.

'Do you call that serious?' he said.

'Certainly, half of it belongs to you.'

'Do me the favour to say no more about it. Father only meant to have one heir and we are carrying out his wishes.'

'No, I cannot accept.'

Gaston, thinking that his brother looked annoyed, said:

'You must be very rich or think I am very poor, to insist like this?'

'I am neither rich nor poor,' Louis replied, after hesitating, for it was an awkward question to answer without committing himself.

'I should be pleased if you were as poor as Job to share with me all I have.'

After breakfast Gaston said:

'Come and have a look round my, or rather our, property.'

The suspicions of Louis were somewhat aroused, for his brother seemed to avoid so obstinately the confidences he was trying to obtain.

They examined the house and iron foundry together, and the sight of such a fine place reawakened in Louis that feeling of jealousy which had been dormant for twenty years. He compared in his mind the position of Gaston, who was rich, honoured and happy, with his own.

After the inspection Gaston, the novelty of whose new property had not yet worn off, asked his brother what he thought of it.

'I think,' he replied, 'that you have, in the midst of the most beautiful country in the world, a lovely place to tempt a poor Parisian.'

'Ah well, brother,' Gaston said, 'since it is mine, it is yours as well. Leave foggy Paris and come here and live beneath the beautiful sky of Bearn. With our capital we can work wonders. Does my plan suit you?'

Louis was silent. A year ago he would have joyfully accepted the offer, but now he had an accomplice he could not leave Paris and abandon his scheme.

'You give me no answer,' Gaston insisted in surprise; 'do you see any objection to my plan?'

'Without my salary,' Louis replied, 'from a post I occupy in Paris, I should not have enough to live upon.'

'That is your objection is it? and yet a minute ago you offered me half your inheritance. Either you have misunderstood me, Louis, or you are a bad brother.'

Louis bent his head. Gaston had involuntarily touched an open wound.

'I should be a burden to you,' Louis murmured.

'A burden! You are mad. Did I not tell you I was rich? Do you think you have seen all I possess? This is only a fourth part of my wealth. Do you think I should risk the savings of twenty years in an enterprise like this? I have an income of 24,000 francs from investments, and my property in Brazil is being sold. I have already received 400,000 francs for part of it. The money is with my banker in Paris.'

'Who is he? One of your friends?' Louis asked, trembling with pleasure, for he would find out now how far he was threatened.

'No, he was recommended to me by my banker at Pau as a very rich, prudent and straightforward man. His name is Fauvel, and his address Rue de Provence. Do you know him?'

'By reputation, yes.' Louis replied, turning pale and then blushing, though he was prepared for the name.

'We will make his acquaintance together, shortly, for I will accompany you when you return to Paris to settle up your business affairs before coming here to live.'

'Oh! Are you coming to Paris?' Louis said, endeavouring to appear undisturbed at this plan which, if carried out, would be his ruin.

'I detest Paris, but I understand that Mademoiselle de la Verberie lives there and I wish to see her again. I can tell you the reason, too. I entrusted our mother's jewels to her charge.'

'And after twenty-three years you want to reclaim them?'

'Yes, or rather no; that is only a pretext. I want to see her because I loved her.'

'How will you find her?'

'Oh, that will be simple. Anyone in the country will tell me her husband's name. I will write to Beaucaire tomorrow.'

Louis made no answer; he was confronted with an unforeseen situation and he did not care to say anything before calculating its possible consequences.

For the rest of the day Louis carefully avoided discussing his brother's plans, but at night when alone in his room, he faced the situation which at first seemed desperate.

During the twenty years he had spent at war with society he had been in some tight places, and had always managed to escape. But now he was without ideas and confidence and his natural impudence seemed to have forsaken him.

He asked himself whether it would not be wise to borrow a large sum off his brother and disappear.

Could any human means prevent the meeting between Valentine and Gaston? Apparently not. Danger seemed to threaten from every side; from Madame Fauvel, her niece, and the banker; Gaston, too, if he discovered the truth would take his revenge; and even his accomplice Raoul would turn upon him in case of failure.

'I can do nothing,' Louis said to himself, 'but gain time and wait for my opportunity.'

The next morning he was affectionate, gay, and much more talkative than before. His object was to keep Gaston occupied and amused, and keep his mind from Paris and Valentine. He hoped to demonstrate to his brother how useless and painful it would be for him to see Valentine, and if Gaston persisted, he would volunteer to undertake the delicate mission of reclaiming the jewels himself. He soon recognized the futility of his efforts and hopes, for one day Gaston said:

'I have written to Lafourcade at Beaucaire to find out the name of Valentine's husband.'

'You have not given up the idea of seeing her then? Have you thought that now she is another man's wife she might refuse to see you? You will disturb her life and cause her regrets.'

'I am foolish, I know,' Gaston replied, 'but my folly is very dear to me.'

From the way he said this Louis could see that his brother would never change his mind. From this time he was very careful either to meet the postman or else look at the letters before his brother.

The following Sunday a letter came with the Beaucaire postmark, and Louis promptly pocketed it. On opening it he found it was the expected letter, signed Lafourcade. The letter contained the information required, and also a request that as the writer did not know M. Fauvel and wanted to see him on his approaching visit to Paris, he might use Gaston's name.

Louis trembled like a man who has escaped a great danger. But his interception of the letter would only give him a respite of twelve days at the most. His brother would wait another week or so for a reply and then write again to Lafourcade, who would be surprised and reply at once.

He made up his mind that the only thing to be done was to borrow a good round sum from his brother and escape to America, and leave Raoul to do the best he could. He was sorry that the most beautiful scheme of his life was a failure, but what was the use of fighting against destiny?

The following day Louis was waking arm in arm with his brother and had started on a little story, the end of which would have been a loan of 200,000 francs, when a young fellow dressed as a workman passed and saluted them. It was Raoul de Lagors.

Louis was overwhelmed with surprise; so great was the shock that Gaston noticed him tremble and asked the reason. He excused himself by saying that he had hurt his foot with a stone. He walked by his brother's side and answered his questions automatically without knowing what he was saying.

Why had Raoul come to Oloron? Had something unexpected happened in Paris?'

Since he had been at Oloron, Louis had written to Raoul almost every day without receiving any answer.

Gaston retired early that evening and his brother lit a cigar and went out. He had hardly gone a hundred yards before Raoul stepped from a copse and stood in front of him.

'What are you doing here?' Louis asked him. 'Are we in any danger?'

'No, everything is going on well.'

'Then what are you doing here? Why have you left your post at the risk of ruining our plans?'

'That,' Raoul said quietly, 'is my business.'

Louis seized his wrists, but Raoul freed them without an effort and taking a revolver from his pocket, said provokingly:

'Gently! gently! I don't like being hurried, and I have an answer for you here. But don't think you are going to frighten me. I will answer you, but not here on the high road and in the moonlight.'

Raoul led the way across the fields till they were some distance from the road. 'Now, dear uncle,' he began, 'I will tell you my reason for coming. I have received your letters and read them over several times. You meant to be prudent, I know, but you were so obscure that I could not understand them. The only clear thing in them is that we are threatened by great danger. But before facing the danger I want to know what it is.'

'But I told you to make your mind easy.'

'Then, dear uncle, I must have entire confidence in you.'

'Certainly. Your doubts are absurd after all I have done for you. What would have become of you if I had not fetched you from London? Who is working now to secure your future? Why I am.'

'Superb,' Raoul interrupted, 'magnificent, splendid! Of course you did not need me when you fetched me? But go on proving that you are the most disinterested of uncles.'

Clameran kept silence for fear of giving way to his anger.

'I have come,' Raoul went on, 'because I know you. I have just as much confidence in you as I ought to have. If it was to your advantage to ruin me you would do so. In case of danger you would think of yourself, not of your dear nephew. Do not protest, it is quite natural, and I should do the same if I were in your place. Only take care; I am not to be played with. But let us leave off quarrelling and get to business.'

Louis understood, and told briefly and clearly what had happened since he had been with his brother. He, however, made out his brother's fortune to be much smaller than it really was.

When he had finished Raoul said:

'Well, we are in a mess. But you think we shall get out of it?'

'Yes, if you do not betray me.'

'I have never betrayed anyone yet, Marquis. But what are you going to do?'

'I don't know, but I shall find a way. You can go back to Paris without any risk as long as I am here watching Gaston.'

'Are you sure,' Raoul said, 'there is no risk?'

'Yes! Madame Fauvel will never dare to raise her voice against us.'

'That is true,' Raoul replied very seriously; 'but she is not the person of whom I am afraid. It is Madeleine who is our implacable enemy. You despise her, but you are mistaken. She is strong; she is capable of the most audacious plans, and misfortune will give her experience. She loves Prosper, she has not given up hope, and the woman who loves defends her love like a tigress her cubs. The danger is there.'

'She has a dowry of 500,000 francs.'

'That is true, and at five per cent that is an income of 12,500 francs each; but if you are wise you will give up the idea of marrying her.'

'Never! never!' Clameran cried. 'I would still marry her if she were poor. I love her.'

Raoul was astonished at his uncle's declaration; he stepped back and raised his arms in immense surprise.

'Is it possible that you love Madeleine?'

'Yes,' Louis replied; 'is it so extraordinary?'

'No. Only this passion explains your surprising variations of conduct. If you love Madeleine we must give up our scheme.'

'Why?'

'Because, uncle, when the heart is lost, so is the head. A day will come when you will betray us for a smile.'

Louis interrupted his nephew with a peal of forced laughter.

'Do you hate beautiful Madeleine?' he said.

'She will be our ruin. It is her dowry that I love.'

'Well, then, why do you complain? You will have half the dowry without the woman. But still we agreed on the day I took you away from the most frightful misery that I should be master.'

'Yes; but you forget that my life or liberty at least are upon the game. Hold the cards, but let me advise you how to play them.'

The accomplices discussed the situation till after midnight, and then arranged to meet at the same time on the following evening. 'By which time,' Louis said, 'I shall have thought out a plan. But above all be careful here.'

'My costume,' Raoul replied, 'ought to have told you that I do not mean to show myself. I have arranged in Paris so ingenious an alibi that I defy anyone to prove that I have left my house at Vésinet, and I also travelled third class. But good-night! I must go back to my inn.'

Louis de Clameran returned to his brother's house in a very uneasy frame of mind. He was distrustful of his accomplice. The precautions Raoul had taken before leaving Paris aroused his suspicions, and Louis realized that the letters he had written to him from his brother's house placed him entirely at his mercy. 'Perhaps,' he thought, 'his intention is to revolt, get rid of me, and take all the profits of our enterprise!'

The following day Louis, after a sleepless night, was so preoccupied that his brother noticed and several times asked the cause of his abstraction. But at last the evening came and he could meet Raoul. He found him in the same field as the previous night.

'Well,' Raoul asked, 'have you made up your mind?'

'Yes; I have two plans, both of which I think are certain to succeed. The first depends upon your acceptance. What do you say to abandoning the affair altogether? Would you consent to disappear and leave France if I gave you a good round sum of money?'

'How much?'

'I can give you 150,000 francs.'

'Beloved uncle,' he said, 'I am sorry you do not know me. You shuffle and dissimulate with me, which is neither generous nor clever; it is not generous because in so doing you are breaking our agreement; nor is it clever, because I am as strong as you. If you offer me 150,000 francs like this I am sure you will obtain a million francs for yourself.'

Clameran made a gesture of protest.

'You are talking nonsense,' he said.

'No, I am judging the future from the past. I have hardly received a tenth part of the money I have drawn from Madame Fauvel, often against my will.'

'But we have a reserve fund.'

'Which is in your hands, dear uncle. If the game was up, tomorrow you would take flight with the money, while I, who was without money, would fall into the hands of the police.'

'Ungrateful wretch!' Louis murmured.

'Shall I prove that you are deceiving me?' Raoul asked.

'If you can.'

'Very well. You told me your brother was fairly well off, did you not? Ah, well, Gaston has an income of 60,000 francs at the very least. The property here is worth 300,000 francs, and he has 400,000 francs to the credit of his account with

M. Fauvel, which makes a total of 700,000 francs. But besides all this he has authorized the purchase of more property. You see I have not wasted the day.'

Louis made no answer.

'You had,' Raoul went on, 'the finest scheme in the world, and now it seems to be ruined largely by your own fault.'

'Events cannot be regulated to suit one's purpose.'

'Yes, when a man is strong. Fools trust to luck, while the wise prepare. When you found me in London we agreed to ask my dear mother to help us, and be charming to her if she agreed with a good grace. But at the risk of killing the goose which lays the golden eggs you have tormented the poor woman so as to almost drive her mad.'

'It was prudent to make haste.'

'Yes; but was that the reason you made up your mind to marry Madeleine? Then it became necessary for her to be in the secret. She is incensed against us, and I shall not be surprised if she confesses to M. Fauvel or informs the police. You say you love her, but that is nothing. You embarked upon this business without sufficient knowledge. Why did you tell me that my father was dead? He is alive, and now we have acted so that I cannot make myself known to him. He is rich and would have made me so, but now I shall not have a halfpenny. He is going to look for Valentine, and when he finds her the game is up.'

Louis interrupted Raoul with a severe gesture.

'That will do,' he said. 'I have a plan to save the situation.'

'What is it?'

'That is my secret,' Louis replied.

They were both silent for a moment and then both shuddered, for the same terrible thought had occurred to them both and they understood one another.

Louis was the first to break the silence.

'Then you refuse,' he said, 'the 150,000 francs to disappear?'

'Yes, I will go for a large fortune. I will succeed or perish with you.'

'And you will obey me?'

'Blindly.'

Raoul asked no more questions as to his accomplice's plan, so he must have been sure he had guessed right.

'First of all,' Louis said, 'you must go back to Paris, and be more attentive than ever to Madame Fauvel. Cast the blame of all your past conduct upon me. The more odious you make me look in the eyes of Madame Fauvel and Madeleine, the greater the service you render me. We must appear to have had a deadly quarrel, and if you still continue to see me when I return to Paris, it is only because you cannot help it.'

'What!' Raoul cried in surprise; 'You adore Madeleine, and this is how you try to please her? I don't understand.'

'Have you ever heard,' Louis asked, 'of the man who would set fire to his house in order to have the right to clasp in his arms the woman he loved?'

'Yes.'

'Well, at the right moment I will, morally, set fire to Madame Fauvel's house, and rescue her niece in that way. The more they hate and despise me now, the more beautiful will my action seem then. Patience will avail me nothing, but a sudden change will make me appear like an angel.'

'Not at all bad,' Raoul said when his uncle had finished.

'Then you quite understand,' Louis said. 'Let me know if there is any news in Paris and I will write to you, and keep your eye on the cashier.'

'Prosper! Oh there is no danger from that quarter. He is my best friend.'

They shook hands and separated as friends, though in reality they were deadly enemies.

Raoul had not forgiven his uncle for trying to play with him, while Louis was frightened at his nephew's attitude. He was not hurt by his nephew's reproaches, but cut to the quick of his vanity at being humiliated by a child. For the moment he was very much afraid of his young accomplice and wrote long letters to him according to promise, but a time would come when Raoul would be no longer necessary to him, and then he would ruin him.

Gaston seemed to have forgotten that he had written to Beaucaire, so absorbed was he in his new enterprise. Five days after Raoul's departure he became suddenly unwell. He was seized with vertigo and dizziness.

'I have often had these attacks,' he said, 'at Rio. A couple of hours' sleep will cure me. Wake me at dinner-time.'

But at dinner-time he was worse. A frightful headache had come on. His temples throbbed, and there was a feeling of constriction and dryness at his throat. His tongue would not obey his thoughts. If he wished to pronounce a word he said another instead, a symptom to be found in certain cases of dysphonia and alalia. Then all his maxillary muscles stiffened and he could only open and shut his mouth with a painful effort.

Louis wished to send for a doctor, but his brother was opposed to the idea.

'The doctor,' Gaston said, 'will drug me and make me ill, and I know the remedy for this malady.'

He ordered Manuel, an old Spaniard who had been in his service for ten years, to prepare some lemonade.

The next morning Gaston seemed much better, for he got up and ate a good breakfast. But at the same time as the previous evening the pains came on more violently than before. Louis sent for a doctor without consulting his brother. The doctor said it was nothing serious and gave him some medicine.

But in the night the course of the malady abruptly changed. The earlier symptoms gave place to a terrible oppression which caused the patient to keep turning in bed without being able to find an easy position.

When the doctor came the next morning he seemed surprised and disconcerted at the change, and asked Manuel whether he had given his master a larger dose of morphia than he had prescribed. The servant replied that he had not. The doctor gave Gaston some different medicine and went away, saying that he would come again the next morning.

Gaston, realizing that he was very ill, sent for a friend who was a lawyer, for he wished to sign a fresh will leaving the whole of his property to his brother.

The lawyer suggested that if a deed were signed by Gaston associating his brother with him in his business, and acknowledging the receipt of a sum of money equivalent to half his fortune, and he were to die, Louis would only have to pay duty on the remainder of his estate, that is to say half of it.

Gaston adopted the suggestion very readily, for it gave him, if he lived, the chance of sharing his property with his brother without wounding the latter's susceptibilities.

The deed was drawn up, but Louis, whose signature was indispensable, seemed to oppose the idea with all his strength. At last, after a long and heroic resistance, which displayed his noble character and disinterestedness to the best advantage, he consented to sign the document after the doctor had urged him to do so.

Louis was filled with strange sensations when he realized that, whatever happened, he was the legitimate possessor of an income of 25,000 francs, besides other interests. He had never hoped or dreamt of being so well off. But it had come too late for him to enjoy it in peace.

This fortune, which had fallen from the sky, filled his heart with sorrow and anger. It was the most cruel punishment he could imagine for his past life. But far from admitting that he was justly punished, he made Gaston responsible for the horror of his position. His letters to Raoul gave expression to his thoughts.

'I have an income of 25,000 francs,' he wrote, 'and I possess 500,000 francs. A year ago half or a quarter of this sum would have made me the happiest of men, but what use is this fortune today? All the gold in the world will not remove one of the difficulties from our path. We are launched upon such a steep slope now that we must go to the bottom. To try to stop would be madness. Rich or poor, I must still tremble as long as an interview between Gaston and Valentine is possible. How can I prevent it?'

Gaston got little better till the end of the week, when he had two days' freedom from his malady. He got up, ate a little, and walked a short distance, but he looked ten years older.

'Old trees die,' he said, 'when they are transplanted, and I shall do well if I wish to live long to get back to Brazil.'

'Yes,' Louis replied eagerly, 'and I will accompany you. A voyage to Brazil with you would be a holiday for me.'

But the following day Gaston had changed his mind. He would never leave France. He would, as soon as he was better, visit Paris, consult the doctors there, and find Valentine.

Gaston was astonished at receiving no answer from Beaucaire. He wrote again, but his second letter Lafourcade never received. The same evening Gaston got worse and the doctor showed his anxiety. A fatal termination seemed probable.

On the morning of the fourteenth day of his illness Gaston revived. He sent for a priest and remained alone with him for half an hour. Then he called in his workpeople and wished them good-bye. When they had gone he wished his brother good-bye, after making him promise to retain the iron foundry, and as the clock struck twelve he expired.

Now Louis was actually Marquis de Clameran and a rich man. A fortnight later, after settling business matters, Louis wired to Raoul and took train to Paris.

CHAPTER XIX

Raoul, while Louis was at Oloron, had set to work to win back the heart of Madame Fauvel. It was a difficult task, but he succeeded.

During the month Louis was away Madame Fauvel experienced wonderful happiness. Her son Raoul's love overwhelmed her like an adulterous passion; it had the same violence, trouble and mystery. He was more like a young lover to her than a son.

While Madame Fauvel was in the country she had in her husband's absence the whole day at her disposal. This she often spent at Vésinet with Raoul, and afterwards he frequently dined and spent the evening with her. She forgave him his past faults, or rather attributed them to Clameran, while even prudent, suspicious Madeleine admitted that perhaps she had been unjust to him.

Money was a subject never mentioned now, for this excellent son seemed to live on nothing.

By the time that Louis arrived from Oloron Raoul had triumphed.

Louis, though very rich now, resolved to make no apparent change in his style of living. He took up his residence at the *Hôtel du Louvre* as in the past. A carriage driven by Manuel, Gaston's old servant who had remained in his service, was his only fresh expense.

Louis' dream now was to take rank with the great business men in France. He was much prouder of being an ironmaster than a Marquis. He knew that his past would be forgotten. He decided to utilize Raoul for the present.

The first interview between the two accomplices after Louis' return to Paris was a stormy one. It took place at the

Hôtel du Louvre. Raoul, who was a practical fellow, thought the results obtained satisfactory and that it would be foolish to pursue their advantage further.

'We have all we want,' he said to his uncle. 'Let us divide the spoil and retire.'

This did not suit Louis.

'I am rich,' he replied, 'but I have other ambitions. I want to marry Madeleine. I have sworn to do so.'

'If you pursue Madeleine, uncle, you run great risks.'

'Very well. I mean to run them. I will divide with you on the morning of my wedding. Madeleine's dowry will be your share.'

'How are you going to explain your access of wealth?' Raoul asked.

'Oh, easily. To the banker, his wife and Madeleine the Clameran of Oloron will be a natural son of my father's—consequently my brother, born at Hamburg, whom I recognized while I was abroad. It is quite reasonable for him to wish to enrich our family, is it not? You can tell your mother that story tomorrow.'

'It is audacious.'

'How?'

'They may try to verify your story.'

'Who? The banker? Why should he? I am the heir, my title is clear; he pays me and it is all over; neither Madame Fauvel nor her niece will make inquiries for fear of compromising themselves.

Raoul reflected, but he could think of no further objection.

'Very well,' he said, 'I will obey you, but there is no further need for me to draw upon Madame Fauvel's purse now that you are rich.'

'Ah, well,' Louis cried in triumph, 'have you not said sufficient about me for me to refuse you my assistance? I have foreseen everything, and when I explain my plan you will see that we shall succeed.

'Now listen,' he said to Raoul, 'while I explain it to you. I had the first interview with Madame Fauvel to demand her money or her honour. I frightened her and inspired in her the greatest hatred for me. Then you appeared upon the scene and captured her heart. That was the first act of the comedy. In the second act we changed places. Though Madame Fauvel still adored you, your excesses and extravagance frightened her. Then she turned to me for assistance.'

'Poor woman!'

'I did very well,' Louis continued, 'in that part. I was grave, cold and paternal. I triumphed at your expense. Madame Fauvel loved and esteemed me. In act three Madame Fauvel, with Madeleine's assistance, found out our real worth. She feared and despised us both, and only a mother's heart prevented her from hating you with all her strength. A mother can at the same time despise and adore her son.'

'She made me understand it in terms which moved even me.'

'When Gaston's existence was revealed to us the position was: Madame Fauvel was terrified, and Madeleine had dismissed Prosper and promised to marry me. Since then you have redeemed your character in Madame Fauvel's eyes and blackened mine. She admires your noble character again, and in the eyes of both I am the pernicious influence which corrupted you.'

'Quite right, uncle, that is the present position.'

'Well, for the fifth act we must have a change of scene. Tomorrow you must go to see Madame Fauvel and tell her the story we agreed upon about Gaston. She will not believe you, but you yourself must appear convinced of the truth of your story. In four or five days' time I will see M. Fauvel and confirm my Oloron solicitor's letter to the effect that the funds in his charge belong to me. I will tell the "natural brother" story to him and ask him to retain the money. It will be for you a guarantee of my sincerity.'

'We will talk of that presently.'

'After that, my fine nephew, I will go to Madame Fauvel and tell her that when I was poor I had to ask her to aid her son, but now that I am rich I am going to take charge of Raoul's future.'

'Do you call that a plan?'

'You will see. At that declaration Madame Fauvel will probably feel inclined to embrace me, but the thought of her niece will stop her. She will ask me if I will give up the thought of marrying her niece. I shall reply "no", and then that will give me a fine chance of displaying my disinterestedness.

'You thought me mercenary, madame, I shall say, but you are mistaken. I have been captivated by the grace and charm of Mademoiselle Madeleine and I love her. Were she penniless I would go down on my knees and ask for her hand. It has been agreed that she shall be my wife, and I must insist on it being carried out. My silence is the price of it, and to prove that it is not her dowry I want, on the day of my marriage I shall make over to Raoul securities to produce an income of 25,000 francs.'

Louis had delivered this speech with so much feeling that Raoul was delighted, and cried out:

'Splendid! The gift of a fortune to me will probably bring mother over to our side.'

'I hope so,' Louis went on, 'and all the more because I shall furnish her with good excuses. I shall prove to Madame Fauvel and her niece that Prosper has unworthily abused them. I will show them that he is overwhelmed with debt, a rake, a gambler and living openly, so they say, with a courtesan.'

'Don't forget to say that Gypsy is attractive; that will crown it all.'

'Then I shall tell Madame Fauvel that if she really loves her niece she ought to wish to see her married to an important man, a great manufacturer, the heir of one of the finest names in France, who is rich enough to give her a good position in the world, rather than to a penniless cashier.'

'If you don't convince her,' Raoul said, 'you will make her hesitate.'

'After that,' Louis went on, 'I shall disappear and your part will begin. Your mother will repeat our conversation to you, but at the idea of accepting anything from me you will revolt. You will declare that you will die of hunger rather than accept anything from a man you hate. This noble sentiment, however, will not prevent you resuming your life of dissipation. You will press her for money pitilessly, and whatever you get will be your own, I shall take no share of it.'

'In that case I shall move quickly.'

'That is what I want you to do. You must in less than three months exhaust the entire resources of these two women. They must be absolutely ruined, without money, without jewellery.'

'Do you hate these unfortunate women?' Raoul asked.

'Hate them?' Louis cried, 'hate them! Don't you see that I love Madeleine madly.'

'And yet the idea of preparing all this trouble for her does not move you?'

'It is necessary. She would never be mine without. The day you drive Madame Fauvel and her niece so near the abyss that they can see the bottom I shall appear. When they believe that they are lost beyond redemption, I will save them. I shall put so much nobility and grandeur into the great scene that Madeleine will be touched. When she sees that it is her person not her money I desire, she will cease to despise me. I do not say she will love me, but she will give herself to me without repugnance, and that is all I ask.'

'You will certainly oust Prosper, uncle,' Raoul said, 'but his remembrance will always be between you and Madeleine.'

An evil smile lit up Louis' face.

'In six months,' he went on, 'she will love him no longer. When it suits me I shall complete his destruction. He has a costly mistress, and one day he will need money to pay his gambling debts, and he is a cashier.'

Raoul could not help protesting.

'Oh!'

'Yes, I know he is honest,' Louis went on, 'so am I. Prosper annoys me, and with your help I shall get him into such a scrape that he will give up even the thought of Madeleine.'

'You have reserved,' Raoul interposed, 'a fine part for me.'

'What! My nephew with scruples?'

'Not exactly scruples; but still—'

'You want to draw back? You want all the delights of wealth and you want to remain virtuous. For that a man needs to be born wealthy.'

'I have never been rich enough,' Raoul replied humbly, 'to be honest, and now it seems very hard to torture two defenceless women and destroy a poor devil who calls himself my friend.'

This continued resistance made Louis lose his temper.

'Well,' he cried, 'I feel sorry for you. A glorious opportunity presents itself for us to make our fortunes at one stroke and you rebel. No one but an ass would do it. You would rather live on an occasional thousand franc note from Madame Fauvel, then?'

'I am neither ambitious nor cruel.'

'Supposing Madame Fauvel were to die tomorrow, what would become of you then?'

Raoul angrily interrupted his uncle:

'That will do,' he said, 'I never meant to back out. I only wished to show you what infamy you expected of me, and to prove to you that without me you can do nothing. Now, uncle, what do you offer me in case of success?'

'I have already told you, an income of 25,000 francs and all the money you can get between now and the date of my marriage.'

'What guarantee are you going to give me?'

The accomplices knew each other and distrusted each other, but after a long discussion matters were arranged to their mutual satisfaction and they separated with a handshake.

Everything happened as Louis de Clameran had foreseen. Madame Fauvel had just begun to breathe more freely when Raoul's conduct abruptly changed. His extravagances increased and never had he been so pitiless and exacting in his demands for money.

In a month Raoul exhausted the resources of Madame Fauvel and her niece. They kept the tradespeople waiting for their accounts. For months they had bought nothing for themselves, but they pretended to make many costly purchases and even prepared fictitious bills.

Madeleine, who was more far-sighted than her aunt, could see that the time was fast approaching when they would have to say 'No' to Raoul, and everything would be discovered. She realized the uselessness of their sacrifices, but kept silent. She even said to her aunt:

'When Raoul is sure that we can do no more for him, he will stop.'

At last the time came when Raoul pretended that he had never before been in such a fix and must have 2,000 francs.

'I have nothing left but my jewels,' Madame Fauvel replied in despair. 'Take them if they are any use to you.'

Raoul could not help blushing at his own impudence. He felt sorry for this poor woman, but the thought of the fortune which awaited him urged him on. In a brutal voice he answered his mother:

'Give them to me; I will pawn them.' One by one all the jewels of Madame Fauvel and Madeleine were pawned.

Towards the end of November, Madame Fauvel felt that she was on the eve of a catastrophe, and it occurred to her to consult the Marquis, whom she had not seen since he had come to announce his accession of wealth on his return from

Oloron. After some hesitation she consulted Madeleine, who, to her great surprise, approved and urged her to lose no time.

Madeleine, judging it impossible that Raoul would run the risk of losing everything without a secret motive, had come to the conclusion that the persecution was more feigned than real, and that its object was to force her aunt to apply to the Marquis. She had divined this from certain glances the Marquis had fixed upon her, and as she had made up her mind to sacrifice herself, anything seemed preferable to the life Raoul was leading them.

The following morning Madame Fauvel, who had previously sent the Marquis a note, called upon him at the *Hôtel du Louvre*. He received her with frigid and studied politeness. He appeared annoyed at his nephew's conduct, and when Madame Fauvel told him of his ceaseless demands for money, Clameran seemed dumbfounded.

'Oh!' he cried, 'what dreadful audacity. In four months I have myself given him 20,000 francs, simply because he threatened to apply to you.'

Seeing the look of surprise and doubt on Madame Fauvel's face, the Marquis took out a bundle of Raoul's I.O.U.s, which amounted to 23,500 francs.

Madame Fauvel was overwhelmed.

'He has had,' she said, '40,000 francs from me as well, so he has spent at least 60,000 francs in four months.'

'It would be incredible,' Clameran replied, 'if he were not, as he says, in love.'

The Marquis seemed to pity Madame Fauvel and promised to see Raoul the same evening and remonstrate with him. Then after much protesting he placed his entire fortune at her disposal.

Madame Fauvel refused his offer, but she was touched by it, and on her return said to her niece:

'Perhaps we have made a mistake, perhaps he is not a scoundrel after all.'

Madeleine shook her head, for the Marquis' fine disinterestedness confirmed her presentiments.

Raoul found his uncle radiant when he went to see him.

'Everything is going on splendidly, nephew,' Clameran said; 'you are a fine partner. Forty thousand francs in four months.'

'Yes,' Raoul replied carelessly, 'and I obtained about the same sum on the jewels.'

'You must have saved a lot of money, for I suppose the lady is only an excuse?'

'That, uncle, is my business. You remember our agreement. Madame Fauvel and Madeleine have turned everything into money; they have nothing left, and I have had enough of my part.'

'So your part is ended. You must not ask me for any more money. The mine is laid now, and I am only awaiting an occasion to explode it.'

Louis de Clameran expected his rival Prosper Bertomy to furnish this occasion himself. He had sworn to ruin the cashier before marrying Madeleine, but though the latter led a fast life, all attempts to hasten his downfall failed, and it was in vain that Raoul, with his hands full of gold, had played the part of tempter.

Though Prosper gambled heavily, he never lost his head over it, and though his mistress, Nina Gypsy, was extravagant, she was devoted to him, and her extravagance did not go beyond certain limits. His position was not without hope, but to gain time was a necessity.

Raoul, who was his intimate friend, had realized the position, and said to his uncle:

'Do not count upon him making a slip, for he has a clear head. I do not know what he can see in the future; perhaps when he reaches the end of his tether he will commit suicide, but one thing is certain, he will never commit a dishonourable action, or touch the money in his charge.'

'We must urge him on,' Clameran replied, 'lend him money, play upon his vanity, put expensive caprices into Madame Gypsy's head.'

'Uncle,' Raoul said, 'you don't know him. You cannot galvanize a dead man into life. Madeleine killed him the day she dismissed him.'

'We shall see.'

To Madame Fauvel's great surprise Raoul's conduct underwent another marvellous change. He became so parsimonious as before he had been extravagant. On the score of expense he said he wanted to spend the winter at Vésinet. In reality he wished to avoid his mother's visits.

About this time Madame Fauvel got her husband to offer Raoul a post in his bank, but though he was pleased with the idea, Clameran made him refuse.

This refusal annoyed the banker. M. Fauvel's reproaches served Raoul as an excuse to cease his visits, and from that time he only saw his mother in the afternoon when he was sure M. Fauvel was out. His visits, too, were only just frequent enough for him to keep in touch with the affairs of the house.

The sudden quiet after all their agitation appeared very sinister to Madeleine. She realized that it was the calm before the storm.

Raoul had tried in every way to compromise Prosper without success, and Clameran was becoming impatient, when at three o'clock one morning he was awakened by his nephew.

'What is it?' he asked in uneasy tones, for he realized that it must be important for his nephew to come at that hour.

'Perhaps it is nothing, perhaps everything. I have just left Prosper after dining with him, Madame Gypsy and three friends. After dinner we played cards till supper time. At supper, Prosper, who was very drunk, allowed the word by which the safe is locked to escape him.'

Clameran could not help uttering a cry of triumph.

'What is it?' he asked.

'His mistress' name—Gypsy!'

Clameran was so excited that he jumped out of bed and started pacing the room.

'We have him now,' he said, with an expression of satisfied hate, 'we have him. If he won't touch the safe on his own account, we will do it for him. You know where the key is kept, you have told me—'

'When M. Fauvel goes out he leaves it in one of the drawers of the desk in his room.'

'Very well! You must go and ask Madame Fauvel for the key, and if she will not give it you, you must take it by force, open the safe and take the contents. Ah, Master Prosper, loving the woman I love will cost you dearly.'

For nearly five minutes Clameran seemed almost mad with a strange mixture of hatred against Prosper and love for Madeleine, till Raoul, to calm him, said:

'Before rejoicing over the victory, let us examine the difficulties in the way.'

'I see none.'

'Prosper may change the word tomorrow.'

'It is not likely; he will not remember that he mentioned it; besides we have no time to lose.'

'By M. Fauvel's express order only a very small sum of money is left in the safe at night.'

'I can assure a very large sum being left there when I like. I have 300,000 francs to my credit there, and if I give notice that I want to withdraw that sum very early one morning, just after the bank opens, the money will pass the night in the safe.'

They spent many hours discussing the scheme. Raoul feared invincible resistance on Madame Fauvel's part, but Louis did not.

It only remained for the two accomplices to make final arrangements and fix the day for the attempt. They decided after minute reflections and calculations that the robbery should be committed on the evening of Monday February 7. This day was chosen because Raoul knew that on that date M. Fauvel was dining with a financier, a friend of his, and Madeleine was invited to a girls' party, so that, barring accidents, when he called on his mother at half-past eight, he would find her alone.

'This very day,' Clameran concluded, 'I will ask M. Fauvel to have my money ready for me on Tuesday. I know the time is very short, but M. Fauvel is a proud man, and if I say it is very urgent, he will oblige me. You will have to ask Prosper, as a personal favour, to have the money ready when the bank opens.'

'I am entertaining Prosper and Gypsy at Vésinet tonight,' Raoul said, 'and if you will let me know the banker's reply, I will ask Prosper then.'

'I will let you know,' Louis replied.

After breakfasting together, they separated in high spirits, Clameran quite joyful, and Raoul calm and resolute.

Everything was in their favour. The banker consented to the money being withdrawn and Prosper promised to have it ready.

Louis was almost mad at the certainty of his triumph, and counted the hours and minutes.

'After this,' he said to Raoul, 'I shall become an honest man.'

Raoul, on the contrary, became more and more sorrowful. Reflection showed him the hideousness of this atrocious act. This time he had not even the excuse to make himself that he was in danger. He knew that he ran no risk of imprisonment, for even if M. Fauvel learned the truth, he would do his utmost to conceal the disgraceful story.

There was another thing, too, which he had not admitted to Clameran, and which astonished himself. He had a sincere affection for Madame Fauvel. He had been happy at Vésinet while his accomplice was at Oloron. He would have liked to become an honest man, and could not see the use of crime when he was well off. He would have betrayed Clameran, who for the satisfaction of an egoistic passion had abused his power, if he could have done so without ruining himself too.

Louis, however, did not leave his accomplice. He prepared the scene with Madame Fauvel, and made him rehearse it, but Raoul's conscience troubled him, and on Monday evening at six o'clock he was without strength or courage and not sure that he could obey.

Raoul tried to make himself intoxicated but did not succeed, and when the clock struck eight and Louis told him that it was time to start, his face became livid and his teeth chattered. He tried to stand but his legs refused to bear him.

'I cannot do it,' he said.

Louis, who became angry at the thought of the possible failure of his scheme, gave him a glass of port wine and rum mixed, which revived his courage for a few moments, but before Raoul had gone fifty yards along the street he was clinging to Clameran's arm and staggering like a drunken man.

'If I can once get him inside,' Louis thought, knowing Raoul as he did, 'he will be all right, his part will absorb him.'

Louis accompanied him to the door of M. Fauvel's house, and after satisfying himself that Raoul had his revolver, left him to enter.

CHAPTER XX

CLAMERAN had said to Raoul:

'Be very careful how you enter, your appearance ought to tell all that is necessary and avoid impossible explanations.'

This advice was useless, for he was so pale and nervous when he entered the drawing-room that his mother asked him what was the matter.

The sound of her voice acted like an electric shock to him, he shook from head to foot, but he realized that he must play his part.

'This misfortune which has happened to me, mother,' he began, 'will be the last. I am unworthy of you and of a noble and generous father. I have been a madman. Happiness has passed near me, but I could not stretch out my hand to grasp it. Near you was my happiness and I recognize it now that it is too late.'

Madame Fauvel was listening, terrified into silence by the certainty that she was about to hear something very terrible. At last she murmured:

'It is never too late to repent, my son.'

'Oh, if I could!' Raoul cried; 'but it is too late. I am dishonoured and by my own fault. But do not be afraid, mother. I will not drag into the mire the name you have given me. I shall at least have the vulgar courage not to survive my dishonour. But your Raoul will die blessing you and with your name upon his lips.'

'You, die?'

'I must, mother, honour commands me to; I am condemned by judges from whom there is no appeal, my will and my conscience.'

'What have you done?' his mother sobbed out.

'I have played and lost money with which I was entrusted.'

'Is it an enormous sum?'

'No, but you cannot find it. I have already taken all you possess, even to your last jewel.'

'But M. de Clameran is rich and has put his fortune at my disposal. I will go and see him.'

'M. de Clameran is away for a week and tonight my fate is to be decided. Life is sweet at twenty.'

He half drew the pistol from his pocket and added with a forced smile:

'This will settle everything.'

Madame Fauvel was too much beside herself to reflect upon the horror of Raoul's conduct, her one idea was to prevent the suicide of her son.

'Wait till my husband returns, I will tell him I want . . . How much was entrusted to you?'

'Thirty thousand francs.'

'You shall have it tomorrow.'

'I must have it tonight.'

'Why did you not come sooner? Have you no confidence in me? The safe is not open now.'

Raoul was waiting for the word safe and seized upon it with an exclamation of joy.

'The safe!' he cried. 'Do you know where the key is?'

'Yes, it is over there.'

'Give it to me, mother,' he begged.

'Wretch!'

'It is my life that I am asking of you.'

That prayer decided her, she took a candle and got the key, but just as she was going to give it to him she changed her mind.

'No,' she stammered, 'it is impossible.'

He did not insist, but seemed to want to go.

'Then, mother,' he said, 'a last kiss.'

'What will you do with the key, Raoul? Do you know the word with which to open the safe?'

'No, but I can try.'

'But you know that much money is never left in the safe.'

'But still I can try, and if I open it by a miracle and there is money there, God will have taken pity on us.'

'If you do not succeed, will you swear to me that you will wait till tomorrow?'

'By my father's memory, I swear it.'

'Then here is the key.'

Pale and trembling Raoul and Madame Fauvel went down the staircase leading to the business part of the premises. As they went Madame Fauvel had time to reflect, and became convinced that Raoul's attempt would be useless. It seemed to her that it was quite impossible for Raoul to know the word. But even if he succeeded in opening the safe she was certain that he would not find enough money in it.

She was almost reassured as to the consequences of this revolting enterprise, and the thought that Raoul had sworn to wait till the following day was very comforting, for the least delay always brings hope.

By the time they had reached Prosper's room, Raoul had recovered his self-possession. Placing the lamp upon the table he arranged the five buttons of the safe so as to make the word Gypsy. The look of terrible anxiety in his face during the operation aroused his mother's pity.

On his numerous visits to Prosper in his office he had often seen him unlock the safe and had even done so himself. He put the key into the lock and had the safe open in a moment.

Both Raoul and his mother uttered a cry, one of triumph, the other of terror.

'Shut it!' Madame Fauvel cried, frightened at this unexpected result.

She pushed madly at Raoul, seized his arm and pulled it so violently that the key came out of the lock and slid along the safe door, making a long deep scratch.

Raoul saw three packets of notes, which he seized and hid beneath his coat.

Madame Fauvel, exhausted by her effort and the violence of her emotion, had let go Raoul's arm.

'Put back those notes into the safe,' she said, 'I will give you ten times as many tomorrow. My son, have pity on your mother.'

Raoul was not listening; he was examining the scratch, which caused him considerable uneasiness.

'At least,' said Madame Fauvel, 'don't take them all: take enough to save you and leave the rest.'

'What would be the use of that? The robbery will be discovered just the same.'

'Yes, but I will explain everything. I will tell M. Fauvel that I took the money.'

Raoul carefully closed the safe and said to his mother:

'Come along; we must go back, or a servant may go into the drawing-room and wonder what has become of us.'

His cruel indifference and calculation at such a moment filled Madame Fauvel with indignation.

'Ah, well,' she replied, 'so much the better! Then there would be an end to it. André would turn me out, but I should not be sacrificing the innocent. Prosper will be accused of this tomorrow. You have stolen his honour, and Clameran the woman he loved.'

Madame Fauvel was talking so loudly that Raoul was frightened. He knew that a messenger slept in the next room, and though it was not late he might be in bed and listening.

'Let us go upstairs,' he said, seizing Madame Fauvel by the arm, but she resisted and clung to a table.

'I have already been coward enough,' she repeated, 'to sacrifice Madeleine, but I will not sacrifice Prosper.'

'Ah,' Raoul replied with a cynical laugh, 'don't you understand that Prosper and I are in partnership and will divide the plunder?'

'Impossible.'

'Do you think that chance told me the word and filled the safe?'

'Prosper is honest.'

'So am I. But we both want money.'

'You are lying.'

'No, dear mother; Madeleine dismissed Prosper, and now he is consoling himself the best way he can, and consolation is expensive.'

He picked up the lamp and pushed Madame Fauvel towards the staircase. She was too amazed by what she had just heard to resist any longer.

'We must put back the key,' Raoul said, but his mother did not seem to hear him and he had to replace it himself. He carried his mother back into the drawing-room and placed her on a couch, for she was quite prostrate, and her fixed and expressionless eyes frightened Raoul and made him think she had gone mad.

'Come, mother,' he said, 'you have saved my life and rendered Prosper a great service. Don't be frightened; Prosper will be arrested; he will deny it, and as there is no proof of his guilt, he will be released.'

Madame Fauvel could not hear his lies.

'Raoul,' she murmured, 'my son, you have killed me.'

The tones of her voice affected him so, that he felt inclined to replace what he had stolen. But the thought of Clameran stopped him, and fearing someone might come in he kissed his mother and fled.

Clameran, tortured by anxiety, was waiting for his accomplice.

'It is over, uncle, thanks to you,' Raoul said, as he threw the notes upon the table. 'Here is the money which will cost the honour if not the life of three persons.'

Clameran seized them with a feverish hand, saying as he did so:

'Now, Madeleine is mine.'

He handed the notes to Raoul, telling him to keep them as part of his share, and promising him the remainder on the day of his marriage with Madeleine, not before, saying:

'You are too valuable an accomplice to lose, nephew.'

'Very well,' Raoul replied, 'but I will never do another job of the sort.'

'Very well,' Clameran replied with a laugh, 'very well. It is the right time to become honest when you become rich.'

CHAPTER XXI

MADAME FAUVEL remained in a state of torpor for more than an hour, but gradually realized the state of affairs. She could see now that she had been the victim of an odious comedy.

She could not make up her mind whether Prosper was really Raoul's accomplice or not. But even if he were guilty, she excused him and decided that the whole responsibility rested upon herself, because she had been the cause of the ruin of his hopes and love. She made up her mind that Raoul's scheme should be her own secret and be kept even from Madeleine.

When her husband and niece returned Madame Fauvel had managed to conceal all trace of her sufferings and appeared quite calm. But when she tried to get up the next morning she could not do so. Great weakness and pain kept her in bed to await events.

At last Madeleine appeared with a face as pale as death.

'You know what has happened, don't you, aunt?' she said in a harsh voice. 'Prosper is accused of theft and going to be taken to prison. I can see the hand of Raoul and the Marquis in the affair. I know Prosper is innocent, for I have seen him and spoken to him. Had he been guilty, he would not have dared to raise his eyes to me.'

Madame Fauvel groaned. She dared not confess the truth.

'What do these monsters want?' Madeleine went on; 'what further sacrifices will they exact?'

The banker entered almost speechless with fury. 'The rascal,' he cried, 'to dare to accuse me!' Then the banker told them the whole story.

Madame Fauvel made a great effort and got up to breakfast, which was a very sorrowful meal. Afterwards M. Fauvel shut himself up in his private room, but at two o'clock he was informed that the Marquis de Clameran insisted upon seeing him in the public office.

His insistence annoyed the banker, but he went downstairs and found the Marquis standing waiting for him.

'What do you want, sir?' he asked brutally; 'you have had your money, have you not?'

'I have come,' the Marquis said in a tone of deference, 'to offer you my apologies, and I wish to do so in the presence of your employees.'

The banker was taken quite by surprise.

'This morning,' the Marquis, continued, 'I lost my temper. Though my hair is grey, when I am angry I am as violent and inconsiderate as I was at twenty. I bitterly regret my words.'

M. Fauvel could appreciate Clameran's conduct. His anger disappeared at once. Stretching out his hand to the Marquis, he said:

'Let everything be forgotten, sir.'

After a few minutes' friendly conversation, in which Clameran explained his immediate need for the money, he expressed, with some hesitation, his desire to pay his respects to Madame Fauvel.

When the servant announced his name, Madame Fauvel and her niece rose in affright.

While ascending the staircase the Marquis had composed his features, and he looked grave and sad as he bowed to the ladies.

'Excuse me, ladies,' he began, 'from disturbing your sorrow, but I have a duty to perform. I know all.'

Madame Fauvel tried to stop him with a gesture, but he took no notice, and went on addressing Madeleine almost entirely:

'Only an hour ago I learned how, yesterday evening, Raoul, using the most infamous violence, took the safe key from his mother and stole 350,000 francs.'

Madeleine's face turned purple with anger and shame, and seizing her aunt by the wrists she shook her.

'Is it true?' she cried, 'is it true?'

'Alas!' Madame Fauvel groaned.

'And you allowed Prosper to be charged,' she cried, 'and put in prison?'

'Forgive me,' Madame Fauvel murmured. 'I was afraid he was going to kill himself; Prosper and he were accomplices.'

'Oh,' Madeleine cried, 'he told you that and you believed it?'

Clameran judged this to be the right moment to interfere.

'Unfortunately, it is only too true,' he said.

'Proofs, sir! proofs!'

'We have Raoul's confession!'

'Raoul is a scoundrel.'

'But who else could have told him the word? Who left the money in the safe? M. Bertomy.'

'And now,' Madeleine said, making no attempt to conceal her disgust, 'do you know what has become of the money?' There was no mistaking the meaning of her question. It was 'You were the instigator of the robbery and you are the receiver.'

'A day will come, mademoiselle,' he replied, when you will regret treating me so cruelly. I understood the exact significance of your question.'

Clameran took out of his pocket several packets of notes and placed them on the mantelpiece.

'Raoul,' he said, 'has stolen 350,000 francs, here is that sum. It is more than half my fortune. I would willingly give the other half to be sure that this would be his last crime.'

'Thank you, sir,' Madame Fauvel said; 'you are very good.'

Madame Fauvel accepted the restitution as her salvation, but Madeleine, who was too inexperienced to see through Clameran's audacious scheme, still distrusted him. It seemed to her that this disinterestedness was too fine for a man whom she believed to be incapable of a noble sentiment.

'What shall we do with the money?' Madeleine asked.

'Return it to M. Fauvel, mademoiselle.'

'How, sir? To do so would be to denounce Raoul and ruin my aunt. Pick up your money, sir!'

Clameran did so and seemed inclined to go.

'I understand your refusal,' he said. 'It is for me to find a way. But I will not go till I tell you how your injustice has filled me with pain. Perhaps after the promise you deigned to make me, I might have hoped for a different reception.'

'I will keep my promise, sir, after you have given me a guarantee, but not before.'

'Guarantee of what?'

'That after my marriage Raoul will not come and threaten his mother again. I am making a bargain with you. I am giving you my hand in exchange for the honour and life of my aunt.'

'Yes, I will give you a guarantee,' Clameran cried, 'which will make you recognize my good faith. What shall I do to prove my devotion? Shall I try to save Prosper?'

'Thank you for your offer, sir,' Madeleine answered disdainfully. 'If Prosper is guilty, let him suffer; if he is innocent, God will protect him.'

Madame Fauvel and her niece got up to signify that the interview was over. Clameran withdrew.

'What pride and character!' he said to himself. 'But I love her and will humble her to my feet! She is so beautiful.'

Clameran was very angry, for Madeleine's energy, which he had not foreseen, had spoiled his great effect. He realized the impossibility of intimidating her and the dominating influence she possessed over her aunt. Louis had found an adversary in the moment, as he thought, of his last triumph.

The question of the guarantee puzzled him. Once he were married to Madeleine and Raoul were rich, Madame Fauvel would not be troubled again. But how could he demonstrate this to Madeleine? The exact knowledge of all the circumstances of this ignoble and criminal intrigue would have reassured her on this point, but it was obviously impossible to let her know these details before marriage.

Raoul, too, was a source of uneasiness to him, and he was determined to get rid of him; but it was not an easy thing to do.

At last Clameran made up his mind that it was impossible for him to give Madeleine a satisfactory guarantee. He decided that he must wait till Prosper's case had been settled. Then he felt sure Madame Fauvel and Madeleine would soon seek an interview with him.

Madeleine, on the other hand, made up her mind that their enemies would go no further at present, and decided to await events in the meantime by the use of her influence, making her aunt adopt, in her own interest, a firmer and more dignified attitude.

The two women, therefore, concealed their anguish under a mask of indifference. They learned from M. Fauvel the progress of events in the charge against Prosper. They heard of his repeated denials, and Madeleine was sure of his innocence. Madame Fauvel, on the other hand, felt sure of the cashier's guilt and accused him in her own mind of leading Raoul astray.

When Madeleine heard of Prosper's approaching liberation, she asked her uncle for a sum of 10,000 francs for charity. She sent this sum to him with a letter, made up of words cut from her prayer-book, advising him to leave France, for she realized that life would be intolerable to him in his native country. She also realized that she would have to marry Clameran some day, and she preferred the man of her choice to be far away.

Madame Fauvel disapproved of this generosity. She was being pressed for money on every side by her tradespeople, and needed a sum of 15,000 francs to settle their accounts.

To add to their troubles, both Madame Fauvel and Madeleine were compelled to be present at a fancy dress ball given by the Jandidiers. They had no money to pay for their dresses, and their own dressmaker had not been paid for twelve months.

Their new lady's maid, Palmyre Chocareille by name, mentioned, without being asked, a skilful dressmaker who had just started business, and who would make the dresses of such well-known ladies as an advertisement and give them credit.

But they could not go to the ball without their jewellery, and it was all in pawn. Madeleine decided to ask Raoul to devote some of the stolen money to the redemption of part of their jewellery.

The following day she went in a cab to Vésinet to see Raoul on the subject without any suspicion that M. Verduret and Prosper were following her and were witnesses of the interview from a ladder.

Madeleine's attempt was useless. Raoul declared that he had divided the money with Prosper and spent his share, and he was not even willing to give her the pawn-tickets. She insisted, however, and at last obtained those for four or five indispensable articles of small value.

Clameran had ordered Raoul to refuse, and he had only consented after a violent scene, of which Joseph Dubois, Clameran's new servant, was a witness. The Marquis hoped that the women would turn to him in this moment of extreme distress.

There was a great deal of ill-feeling between Raoul and the Marquis now. The latter was trying all he knew to get rid of his accomplice in some way, not dangerous to himself, while Raoul had a presentiment of the other's intention. The only thing to reconcile them was the certainty of a great and imminent danger. This they received at the Jandidier's ball.

They could not guess who the mysterious clown was, who after his transparent allusions to Madame Fauvel, said to Louis in such a strange tone:

'I am your brother Gaston's friend.'

They recognized their danger and after the ball tried to stab him. Raoul tried once more to get Clameran to give up Madeleine.

'No,' he cried, 'I will have her or perish.'

They thought, as they were forewarned, it would be a difficult matter to capture them. But they little knew who was on their track.

CHAPTER XXII

THE DÉNOUEMENT

ALL these facts had been collected and arranged by M. Verduret.

He arrived at Paris at half-past nine in the evening and at once went to the *Hôtel du Grand-Archange*, where he found Prosper impatiently waiting for him.

'Ah,' he said to Prosper, 'now you shall see how far back into the past it is sometimes necessary to go to find the first cause of a crime. If Gaston de Clameran had not gone twenty years ago into an inn at Tarascon your safe would not have been robbed three weeks ago. Valentine de la Verberie has in 1866 paid for the knife thrusts given for love of her in 1840. Nothing is lost or forgotten. Now listen.'

Then he began with the aid of his voluminous notes to tell Prosper the whole story.

During the whole week M. Verduret had scarcely had twenty-four hours' sleep altogether, but he showed no signs of it. Prosper listened to the story, wondering at his lucidity, and recognizing the ingenuity, probability and logic of his explanations, but wondering all the time whether it was really true, or only the dream of an imaginative man.

It was four o'clock in the morning before M. Verduret finished up by saying:

'Now they are upon their guard; they are very clever, but I can laugh at them, I have them fast. In less than a week, Prosper, you will be back in your old place, I have promised your father it shall be so.'

'Is it possible,' Prosper cried, 'that such things take place in Paris?'

'Not only possible, but the real truth. You are young, my friend. You only believe in the horrors of the Assize Court. It is in family circles, often beyond the reach of the law, that real dramas take place. The story I have told you is a commonplace one, but it astonishes you.'

'How could you discover all this infamy?'

The fat man smiled.

'Ah,' he said, 'when I undertake a task I fix my whole attention upon it. A man of moderate intelligence who concentrates his thoughts, all the impulses of his will upon a single aim, is generally successful. Of course a light is needed to guide one in the darkness of such a case, but the flame of Clameran's look when I pronounced his brother's name lit my lantern. From that moment I went straight to the solution of the problem.'

'I would give,' Prosper said, 'anything to know how you arrived at the truth. It is a marvel.'

M. Verduret was flattered by this sincere admiration.

'Very well,' he said, 'I will show you my system. We worked together to try and solve the problem, and you know how I came to suspect that Clameran had something to do with the crime. What did I do then? I placed my agents in the service of the persons I wanted to watch, Joseph Dubois with Clameran, and Nina Gypsy with the Fauvel ladies.'

'I cannot understand how Nina undertook the business.'

'That,' M. Verduret replied, 'is my secret. Having good eyes and ears to look after the present, I wanted to find out about the past, and I went to Beaucaire. The next day I was at Clameran and at once put my hand on the son of Saint Jean the old valet. He is a fine fellow, frank and simple, and he at once guessed that I wanted to buy madder.'

'Madder?' Prosper asked in surprise.

'Certainly. I must tell you I was not just the same as I am now. He had some madder for sale, so we started bargaining. The deal took the whole of the day and we drank a dozen bottles of wine over it. At supper-time Saint Jean, the son, was drunk and I had bought for 900 francs madder which your father will sell.'

Prosper looked so surprised that M. Verduret burst out laughing.

'I had speculated 900 francs,' he went on, 'but I had learned the story of Clameran, the love affair of Gaston, his flight and the fall of Louis' horse. I learned, too, that twelve months before Louis had come back, that he had sold the château to a man named Fougeroux, and that the purchaser's wife, Mihonne, had made an appointment with Louis. The same evening I crossed the Rhône and went to see this woman. Her rascal of a husband has knocked her about so, that she is almost an idiot. I proved to her that I came on behalf of a Clameran and she told me all she knew.'

The simplicity of the investigation overwhelmed Prosper.

'Then,' M. Verduret continued, 'I held the master clue. I had no difficulty in finding out what had become of Gaston. Lafourcade, who is a friend of your father's, told me that he had purchased an iron foundry at Oloron and had died there. Thirty-six hours later I was at Oloron.'

'You are tireless.'

'I believe in striking while the iron is hot. There I met Manuel, who was spending a few days in the neighbour-hood on his way back to Spain, after leaving the Marquis de Clameran's service. From him I had Gaston's exact biography and most minute details of his death. From Manuel I learned of Louis' visit to him, and from an inn-keeper I learned of the arrival about this time of a young workman, in whom I recognized Raoul.'

'But how did you find out about those precious conversations?'

'You think I guessed at them, but you are wrong. My assistants were at work all the time. As they distrusted one another Clameran and Raoul were ingenious enough to keep the letters they exchanged. Joseph Dubois found them, copied most of them, had the most important photographed, and sent it all to me. Nina, too, spent her life listening at doors and sent me an accurate summary of what she heard. I had, too, another way of investigation at the banker's house, which I will let you know about later.'

'I understand,' Prosper murmured.

'And what have you done, my young comrade?' M. Verduret inquired.

Prosper was troubled and blushed. But he realized it would be unwise to conceal the truth.

'Alas,' he replied, 'I was mad. I read in a paper that Clameran was going to marry Madeleine.'

'What did you do?' M. Verduret asked uneasily.

'I wrote an anonymous letter to M. Fauvel, in which I gave him to understand that his wife was deceiving him with Raoul.'

M. Verduret struck the table a violent blow.

'Rascal,' he cried, 'you have probably ruined my plans.'

The fat man's face assumed a threatening expression as he paced the room.

'You are a child, a madman,' M. Verduret said to Prosper; 'had you no confidence in me?'

'You were away, sir; the announcement of the marriage overcame me.'

'Do you know to what risk you expose me? You may be the cause of my failing to keep a sacred oath given to one of the few persons I esteem. But let us try to repair your fault. When did you post the letter?'

'Yesterday evening. I regretted doing so directly it was in the box.'

'What time?'

'Ten o'clock.'

'That means to say that M. Fauvel had your letter in the morning with his correspondence. He was probably alone in his private room when he read it. But tell me as near as possible exactly what you said in the letter.'

Prosper had no difficulty in remembering almost word for word what he had written.

When he had finished M. Fauvel said:

'That was a fine anonymous letter. It leaves everything to be understood, without being precise.

It is vague, sneering and treacherous. Say it over once more.'

When Prosper had finished M. Verduret stood in front of him with his arms folded.

'The effect of your letter,' he said, 'must have been terrible. The banker is a passionate man, is he not?'

'He is violence itself.'

'Then the harm may not be irreparable. I think that every man with a quick temper fears himself and never obeys a first impulse. That is our chance of safety. If M. Fauvel, on the receipt of your letter, rushed into his wife's room crying out: "Where are your jewels?" our prospects are ruined. Madame Fauvel would confess everything.'

'Would that be such a misfortune?'

'Yes, my young friend, because at the first sign of a quarrel between the banker and his wife the birds will fly away.'

Prosper had not thought of that.

'Then,' M. Verduret continued, 'that will cause someone immense sorrow.'

'Someone I know?'

'Yes, comrade. I should be very grieved if these two rascals slipped through our fingers.'

'But you seem to know what you are about.'

M. Verduret shrugged his shoulders.

'Did you not,' he said, 'notice the gaps in my story? The first point is, did Louis de Clameran poison his brother?'

'Yes, I feel sure of it after what you have told me.'

'You are more certain than I dare be. That is my opinion, but what proof have we? I have interviewed the doctor, who is a clever and observant man and not a quack, and he has

no suspicion. I have studied poisons, and I know of none
which produce the effects from which Gaston died.'

'The death was so opportune.'

'That makes it look like a crime. But chance is sometimes
a marvellous accomplice. The second point is that I am
ignorant of Raoul's antecedents.

'Is it absolutely necessary to know them?'

'Yes, but we shall soon know them. I have sent a very clever
friend, M. Palot, to London, and he writes that he is on the track.'

Prosper had left off listening. He had begun to realize that
the guilty would be brought to justice and that he would
marry Madeleine after all. He began to wonder more than
ever at M. Verduret's assistance and the extent of his means
of investigation. What was the cause of his devotion, and
what reward would he require for his services?

The cashier became so excited that he cried out:

'You have no longer the right, sir, to conceal your identity
from me. When a man has been saved and has had his honour
restored to him, he should know whom to thank.'

'Oh! Be patient a few days longer. The business is not
finished yet, nor are you married.'

The clock struck six.

'What?' cried M. Verduret. 'Already six o'clock in the
morning, and I meant to have a good night's rest last night!'

M. Verduret went out of the room and called down the
stairs, 'Madame Alexandré.'

Prosper thought it strange that she was not in bed. She
appeared humble and smiling.

'What can I do for you, gentlemen?' she asked.

'I want,' M. Verduret replied, 'Joseph Dubois and Palmyre
fetched as quickly as possible, and wake me as soon as they
arrive.'

The fat man threw himself down on Prosper's bed, saying
as he did so: 'You don't mind, do you?' and in five minutes
was asleep.

About nine o'clock there were three gentle taps at the door and Joseph Dubois, the Marquis de Clameran's servant, entered out of breath like a man who had been running.

'At last,' he cried, 'sir, you are back. I have not known what to do without you. Yesterday afternoon I sent three telegrams to you—to Lyons, to Beaucaire and to Oloron, and got no answer.'

'There is something doing, then?'

While speaking M. Verduret had arranged his toilette, which had been somewhat disturbed by his sleep. Then sitting down he said to Joseph Dubois, who was still standing respectfully:

'Explain yourself, my man; do it clearly, but as quickly as possible.'

'I don't know your intentions, sir,' he began, 'or your means of action, but you must strike at once.'

'Is that your opinion, Master Joseph?'

'Yes, because if you wait you will find an empty cage and the birds flown. They know there is someone at their heels.'

'What?' M. Verduret cried. 'Someone must have been very clumsy.'

'No, it was not clumsiness,' Joseph went on, 'they have long been suspicious. They suspected something the evening you were disguised as a clown, and the proof of that is that they tried to stab you. However, I think they were beginning to be reassured again till yesterday.'

'Was that the reason you wired to me?'

'Naturally. Yesterday morning about ten o'clock my master began to put his papers in order. At the time I was pretending to lay the fire and watching him. He has an eye like a hawk. He at once realized that someone had touched his papers. He turned pale, and swore.'

'Go on, go on.'

'It is a mystery how he noticed anything. I was so careful to put the things back in their right places. Then he began to examine all the letters one by one. Suddenly he got up with blazing eyes, kicked his chair across the room and rushed at me, crying: "Someone has been at my papers; this letter has been photographed!"'

M. Verduret had become very serious. 'Go on,' he said.

'I was frightened and as a precaution placed a large table between us. While I was wondering how he found out I said to him: "It is not true, sir; you must be mistaken; it is impossible."

'He did not listen to me; he brandished a letter crying: "This letter has been photographed. I can prove it."

'He was quite right. He pointed out a yellow stain made by a drug photographer's use.'

'I know,' M. Verduret interrupted. 'Go on!'

'We had a regular scene. He seized me by the collar and shook me. Then he questioned the porter; but I did not understand that, for it was in English. Finally he seemed pacified. He gave me twenty francs and said: "I am sorry I was rough with you. You are too stupid for a job of the sort."'

'Do you think he meant it?'

'I am positive he did.'

The fat man whistled softly as if to clearly indicate that was not his opinion.

'After it was all over,' Joseph went on, 'the Marquis dressed and went out, taking a cab from the hotel courtyard. He came back about five in good spirits. In his absence I had wired to you.'

'Did you not follow him?'

'Excuse me, sir, one of my friends did, and from him I found out where he went. First of all he went to a stockbroker, and then to the Bank.'

'Is that all?'

'In that direction, yes, sir. But in another the rascals tried to have Mademoiselle Palmyre arrested. Fortunately you had anticipated them.'

Joseph could think of nothing else he had to tell, so he concluded:

'I hope M. Patrigent will rub his hands when I go to see him. He does not guess how Dossier 113 will grow in size.'

After Joseph had finished there was a long silence. Joseph Dubois at last became impatient.

'What shall I do now, sir?' he asked.

'Go back to your hotel, my boy; your master has probably noticed your absence, but he will say nothing to you about it.'

An exclamation from Prosper, who was standing at the window, interrupted M. Verduret.

'Clameran,' Prosper said, 'is over there.' M. Verduret and Joseph rushed to the window and after waiting some time satisfied themselves that Prosper was right. The noble Marquis de Clameran was watching the *Hôtel du Grand-Archange.*

'But still,' M. Verduret said, 'this manoeuvre, daring as it seems, is quite reasonable. He knows that someone is after him and naturally wants to find out who his adversaries are. How his uncertainty must trouble him. Perhaps he thinks it is some of his old accomplices who want to share the spoil. He will stay there till Joseph goes and then make inquiries.'

'But I can go without him seeing me, sir.'

'Yes, I know, you can climb the little wall which separates the hotel from the wine merchant's yard; from there you can go through the stationer's basement, out into the Rue de la Huchette.

'That is it, sir,' he said in surprise. 'I have heard that you know every house in Paris like that. Is it true?'

Prosper was listening all the time with open mouth and watching these men who were fighting so hard and unconcernedly for him.

'There is another way,' Joseph proposed after a little thought. 'I can walk out with my hands in my pockets. After I am gone the Marquis will come and question Madame Alexandré. You can easily tell her what to say.'

'No good!' M. Verduret said decidedly. 'You cannot puzzle such a clever scoundrel in that way, and it will not reassure him. I have a better plan than that. Since Clameran has found out that his papers have been searched, has he seen Lagors?'

'No, sir.'

'He may have written to him.'

'No, I am sure he has not. I have a little system which lets me know when he touches a pen. The pens have not moved for twenty-four hours.'

'Clameran went out part of yesterday afternoon. The man who was following guarantees that he did not write on the way.'

'Then,' the fat man cried, 'forward! I will give you a quarter of an hour to disguise yourself, and keep my eye upon him from here the while.'

Joseph disappeared without a word, and M. Verduret and Prosper remained at the window watching Clameran.

'Why attach yourself thus exclusively to the Marquis?' Prosper asked.

M. Verduret could think of no good reason or likely pretext, so he replied:

'That is my business.'

In less than ten minutes Joseph Dubois reappeared, but there was nothing of the gentleman's servant about him when he did. He looked the part of a junior clerk to perfection. Prosper recognized him now, as the little man who had assisted at the examination of the premises after the robbery. Joseph Dubois had become Fanferlot the squirrel once more.

M. Verduret looked at his subordinate with a satisfied air.

'Not bad,' he approved, 'not bad. There is enough police smell about you to make an honest man tremble. That is how I wished you to be.'

Dubois-Fanferlot was delighted at the compliment.

'Now, sir, what am I to do?' he said.

'Nothing very difficult for a clever man. But the success of my plan depends upon the precision of the manoeuvres. I want to finish with Clameran before turning my attention to Lagors. Now the rascals are separated I want to prevent them rejoining.'

'I understand,' Fanferlot said, 'I am to make a diversion.'

'That is right. You must get out into the Rue de la Huchette and reach the Saint Michel bridge. From there you will descend on to the river bank and take up your position upon one of the quay staircases, in such a way that Clameran can see you from where he is and see that you are watching him. If he does not notice, you are intelligent enough to attract his attention. As soon as he sees you he will become nervous and decamp. You will follow him not very cleverly but tenaciously, and he, recognizing that the police are after him, will do all he can to get rid of you. I don't think he will dare to return to the *Hôtel du Louvre* for fear anyone is there.'

'But if he does return there?' Fanferlot asked.

'I don't think he will do so,' the fat man replied thoughtfully. 'If he has that audacity you must wait for him outside, and follow him again when he comes out. He will probably go by train somewhere, in which case you must follow him to Siberia if necessary. Have you any money?'

'I will get some from Madame Alexandré.'

'Good! I will not examine your account too closely. One word more; if the rascal takes the train anywhere, send word here. Watch him very carefully at night, for he will stick at nothing.'

'Can I shoot?'

'Yes, if he attacks you. Now, my boy, off you go.'

'Why all this trouble?' the cashier murmured. 'I had not so many charges against me as Clameran and I was arrested soon enough.'

'What,' the fat man replied, 'don't you understand even now that I wish to separate the case of Raoul from that of the marquis? But look! The marquis has seen our man.'

Clameran's anxiety was apparent; he took a few steps towards the bridge, then turned right round and went towards the Rue Saint Jacques.

At that moment the door opened and Madame Nina Gypsy, that is Palmyre Chocareille, entered. Each day since she entered Madeleine's service had left its mark on her charming face. Her cheeks were pale, she seemed weighed down by terrible sorrow. After all her happiness she was as humble as misery.

Prosper thought that at the sight of himself Nina would rush to his arms. But she hardly seemed to recognize him and only just ventured to bow. Her attention was fixed upon M. Verduret, like an animal on its master. He was quite paternal and affectionate to her.

'Ah well, my child,' he said, 'have you any news?'

'Yes, I should have been here before to tell you, but I had to get Mademoiselle Madeleine to make an excuse for me to come out.'

'You must thank her for her confidence,' the fat man replied, 'till I can express my gratitude to her in person. I suppose she has remained faithful to our agreement?'

'Yes, sir.'

'They receive the Marquis de Clameran?'

'Yes, now the marriage is settled he comes every evening and Mademoiselle receives him kindly. He is delighted.'

At this Prosper was very angry. He did not understand M. Verduret's plans.

'What?' he cried. 'That wretch, that infernal thief, paying court to Madeleine! What did you tell me, sir, what hopes have you raised in me to keep me quiet?'

With a commanding gesture M. Verduret cut short his complaint.

'That will do,' he said, 'that will do. You are too honest to the very end. If you are incapable of doing anything to help yourself, don't let your childish suspicions interfere with those who are working for you. Have you not already done sufficient to hinder me?'

Turning to Gypsy he said:

'Now, my child, what have you discovered?'

'Nothing positive, but I suspect something. Perhaps it is only a ridiculous presentiment, but it seems to me that there is misfortune hanging over the house, and that the catastrophe is at hand. I can find out nothing from Madame Fauvel, she is like a body without a soul; I could swear that she mistrusts her niece and is concealing something from her.'

'And M. Fauvel?'

'Some misfortune seems to have happened to him. Since yesterday he has been like a madman. Everyone has noticed the change in him. He has become sharp, irritable and nervous. He is like a man restraining himself but ready to burst. I have noticed a strange and terrible expression in his eyes when he looks at his wife. When M. de Clameran came last evening he went out quickly, excusing himself on the plea of business.'

M. Verduret interrupted her with a triumphant expression. He was radiant.

'Ah!' he said to Prosper. 'What did I tell you?'

'Quite right, sir.'

'The poor man is waiting for proof now. Did the ladies go out yesterday?'

'Part of the day.'

'What did M. Fauvel do?'

'He remained at home alone; the ladies took me with them.'

'There is no doubt he sought and found some decisive evidence. Ah, Prosper, your anonymous letter will do us a lot of harm yet.'

M. Verduret's reflections enlightened Madame Gypsy.

'I have it,' she said, 'M. Fauvel knows everything.'

'You mean he thinks he knows the truth?'

'Then I can understand the order which surprised M. Cavaillon so.'

'What order?'

'M. Cavaillon heard M. Fauvel tell his valet, M. Evariste, that under pain of instant dismissal, all letters coming to the house, no matter to whom addressed, were to be brought to him.'

'When was the order given?'

'Yesterday in the afternoon.'

'That was what I feared,' M. Verduret cried; 'it is clear that his mind is made up and he means to have a sure revenge. Shall we be in time to thwart his plans? Can we put a bandage over his eyes thick enough to make him believe in the falsity of the anonymous letter?'

Prosper's folly, perhaps it was excusable, had upset his simple plan, and now he had to find a supreme expedient. He thanked Nina for her information and dismissed her.

Though Nina was dismissed she did not go.

'And Caldas, sir?' she asked timidly.

'I have promised to find him for you,' M. Verduret replied, with a quickly repressed shudder, 'and I will do so; good-bye.'

Three times in a fortnight Prosper had heard this name. The first time was in the corridor at the Prefecture of Police, when a middle-aged man of respectable appearance had whispered it in his ear when he promised him help and protection.

The second occasion, the examining magistrate threw it in his face in connection with Gypsy. He had searched his memory for the name without success.

It was midday and M. Verduret was hungry. He called Madame Alexandré and a meal was soon prepared. For the first time since Prosper had known him, Prosper could see in M. Verduret's face traces of uneasiness and hesitation, and this increased his own anxiety.

'I have put you in a terrible fix, sir,' he ventured to say.

'Yes,' M. Verduret replied, 'terrible is the word. What is to be done? Precipitate events or wait? I am bound, too, by a sacred promise.'

CHAPTER XXIII

THE effect of Prosper's anonymous letter on M. Fauvel had been terrible. It came upon him like a thunderbolt. The thought that his wife deceived him with a man base enough to steal her jewels, for that was what the letter meant, at first stunned him. After a few minutes his reason returned.

'What cowardly infamy,' he cried, 'what shameful abomination! I will think no more about it. I will not soil my mind with it.'

He not only said it, but also thought it. Presently another thought occurred to him.

'Supposing it were true?'

At that thought a fierce wave of anger swept over him, that anger which makes a man lose control of himself and commit crime.

He picked up the letter which he had thrown into the fireplace and examined the writing to see if he could obtain from it any clue to the author. Next he looked at the postmark, but that did not help him either. He could find no clue at all.

He felt sure he ought to ignore it altogether, but after he had thrown it into the fire, perhaps a doubt would remain.

Then he thought of showing it to his wife. But if it were true, if his wife were guilty, that would put her on her guard and destroy any means of investigation and finding out the truth.

The banker at last decided to watch his wife, and collect one by one the proofs of her innocence or guilt. He had, besides, a very simple way of verifying the letter. His wife's diamonds were in pawn, it said. If the letter was wrong in this particular, there was no reliance to be placed upon the rest of it.

While M. Fauvel was still thinking the matter over, and wondering how he could look in his wife's jewel cases without her knowing it, lunch was served. He composed his features and at the table endeavoured by continued talking to prevent his pallor from being noticed.

He took the earliest opportunity to ask his wife if she were going out that day.

'Yes,' she replied, 'the weather is very bad, but Madeleine and I have one or two calls to make.'

'What time do you go?'

'Directly after lunch.'

After the meal was over, the banker retired to his private room, but before doing so he sent his son Lucien out on an errand, for now that his opportunity had come he wished to be alone in the house.

In half an hour's time he heard the sound of carriage wheels and knew that his wife and niece had gone out. Without waiting, M. Fauvel rushed into his wife's room and opened the drawer in which she kept her jewel cases. Many of the cases were missing and those which remained, ten or a dozen, were empty.

The anonymous letter was true.

'No,' he muttered, 'it is not possible.'

Then the thought occurred to him that perhaps his wife had changed her place for keeping them, or sent some to be remounted, so he began to search the room hurriedly, but carefully, leaving no trace behind him.

It occurred to him that his wife had not worn her diamonds at the great ball given by the Jandidiers. He had asked her the reason. She replied with a smile:

'Why should I wear them, as everyone knows them? I shall be more noticeable without them; besides, they don't go very well with my costume.'

Suddenly a ray of hope came into his mind. Perhaps Madame Fauvel's diamonds were in Madeleine's room?

He rushed into his niece's room and searched it too, but found nothing but seven or eight empty jewel cases. She was his wife's accomplice, then!

'They conspired to deceive me,' he murmured. M. Fauvel dropped into a seat, large silent tears flowed down his cheeks, varied only by an occasional deep sigh.

In a moment the edifice of his happiness which had taken twenty years to build, and which he believed to be strong enough to resist the caprices of chance, had been dashed to pieces.

But M. Fauvel's state of prostration did not last long, it was quickly superseded by anger and a desire for vengeance. He quickly realized that the missing jewels were in themselves insufficient evidence. But he could soon procure further proof.

First he called his valet and instructed him to deliver all letters, no matter to whom addressed, to him, the master of the house.

Then he wired to a lawyer at Saint Rémy, asking him to procure him exact information about the Lagors family and Raoul in particular. He then went to the Prefecture of Police to try and get a biography of Clameran. But the police, fortunately for many, are as discreet as the tomb. A magistrate's order is necessary before this information can be given. The banker was politely asked his reasons for wanting to find out about the past of a French citizen, and being unable to give a satisfactory reply, he was advised to apply to the Public Prosecutor.

The banker returned home more angry than ever and found a reply from Saint Rémy awaiting him.

'The Lagors family,' it said, 'is in the greatest distress, and no one knows anything about Raoul de Lagors. Madame de Lagors' children were all daughters and so on . . .'

This revelation was the last drop of water which made the banker's cup overflow. He realized that the infamy and duplicity of his wife was beyond his wildest dreams.

'Wretch,' he cried, mad with rage, 'wretch! She has dared to introduce her lover in the name of a nephew who never existed, in order to keep him in her sight. She has had the shamelessness to introduce him into my house, and I loved him, clasped his hands and lent him money.'

He thought how they must laugh at him when they met, and it seemed to him that death was the only fit punishment for such wretches.

'Now it is my turn to deceive,' he said to himself with frightful satisfaction. At dinner he laughed and joked, but when Clameran appeared about nine o'clock he went out, for fear he could not contain himself.

The following day he was rewarded for his prudence. Among the letters brought to him was one with the Vésinet postmark. Taking infinite precautions he opened it and read:

'DEAR AUNT,

'It is necessary for me to see you today and I am expecting you.

'I will tell you the reasons which prevent me calling upon you.

'RAOUL.'

'I have them now,' M. Fauvel cried, taking a revolver from the drawer and flourishing it.

He believed himself to be alone, but Nina Gypsy, who had returned from the *Hôtel du Grand Archange*, was watching him through the keyhole, and his gestures revealed the truth to her.

M. Fauvel put down the revolver on the shelf, stuck down the letter, and went out to himself take it to the porter, so that his wife should not know that the letter had been through his hands.

He was hardly gone two minutes, but that was long enough for Gypsy, inspired by the imminence of the danger, to enter the room and unload the revolver.

'Ah,' she said to herself, 'the first danger is over, and if I send word of what has taken place by Cavaillon to M. Verduret, perhaps there will be time for him to interfere.'

She sent the message at once.

An hour later Madame Fauvel ordered the carriage and went out. M. Fauvel called a cab and followed her.

'Good God!' Nina thought. 'If M. Verduret does not arrive in time, Madame Fauvel and Raoul are lost.'

CHAPTER XXIV

THE day when the Marquis de Clameran saw that Raoul de Lagors was the only obstacle between himself and Madeleine, he swore he would get rid of him.

The following day Raoul, who was returning home to Vésinet on foot, was attacked by three men. By the exercise of great strength and agility he got rid of them without any more injury than a deep scratch on the left arm.

He decided to be more careful in future and always carry a weapon, but it never occurred to him to suspect his accomplice.

Two days later, however, in a café which he frequented, a big fellow went out of his way to pick a quarrel with him, threw his card in his face and said he was ready to grant him satisfaction.

Raoul wished to rush at him and chastise him there and then, but his friends restrained him.

'Very well,' he said to the fellow, 'be at home tomorrow morning, sir; two of my friends will, call upon you.'

After his anger had cooled a little, he picked up the card and read:

W. H. B. JACOBSON,
Late Volunteer under Garibaldi,
Ex-officer of the Armies of the South (Italy–America)
30, Rue Léone.

'Oh, oh,' Raoul thought, 'he is a fine soldier who has won a bout or two in the fencing school.'

He had a very good idea of the capabilities of those noble heroes who have their military service inscribed upon their visiting cards, but as the insult took place in the presence of numerous witnesses, he asked two of his friends to call upon M. Jacobson early the following morning and come and report to him at the *Hôtel du Louvre*, where he meant to sleep.

After making arrangements he left the café to make a few inquiries as to his assailant. He found that he lived at a doubtful-looking place much frequented by ladies of more than easy virtue, and learned that he was an eccentric gentleman whose only capital seemed to be his military service and a number of expedients of all kinds. He went out often, and returned late and altogether seemed to be a man whose existence was a difficult problem to solve.

These inquiries, and the apparent lack of motive for the quarrel, caused Raoul considerable uneasiness, but he said nothing of the adventure to the Marquis who was still up when he returned to the *Hôtel du Louvre*.

About half-past eight the following morning Raoul's friends came to tell him that M. Jacobson wanted to fight with swords at once in the Bois de Vincennes.

Raoul agreed, and after the encounter had lasted a minute he was lightly touched above the right breast.

The ex-officer wished to continue, but Raoul's seconds declared that honour was satisfied and they would not allow their man to risk his life again.

Raoul was forced to obey them, and he congratulated himself on getting out of the business so well. It struck him, also, that the two attacks upon him formed a singular co-incidence at least, and he began to suspect that Clameran had a hand in both affairs.

Raoul had learned from Madame Fauvel the guarantee which Madeleine had imposed upon the Marquis before she would marry him, and he realized what enormous motive Clameran had to get rid of him.

As soon as this suspicion had entered his mind he recalled a number of insignificant facts, and after a skilful cross-examination of the Marquis, his suspicion became a certainty.

A feeling of anger at the thought of the man whom he had aided seeking his death was followed by one of terror at the thought of his life being threatened by such an audacious scoundrel, and he came to the conclusion that it was better to kill than be killed.

In the days of his misery Raoul would have willingly risked his neck for a few pounds, but with money had come prudence. Now he wished to enjoy his 400,000 francs. He began to try and think of a way to get rid of his accomplice, and while awaiting an opportunity he made up his mind to prevent the Marquis' marriage to Madeleine if possible.

To do that, he knew, would be to cut him to the heart, and he believed that if he freely took the part of Madeleine and her aunt, he would be able to get them out of Clameran's clutches.

That was the reason he wrote to Madame Fauvel and made the appointment with her at Vésinet which she hastened to keep, though she trembled at the thought of his probable demands and menaces.

She found Raoul most charming, a loving son. His object was to reassure her before disclosing his plans. He was on his knees before her saying 'I have caused you so much suffering . . .' when the noise of the door being opened startled him and he got up quickly, to find M. Fauvel standing at the door, revolver in hand.

The banker was terribly pale, and obviously making superhuman efforts to display the cold impassibility of a judge passing sentence upon a criminal.

To the cry of surprise uttered by Madame Fauvel and Raoul when they saw him, he replied, with a nervous grin:

'Ah! You did not expect to see me, did you? You thought my imbecile confidence would allow you perpetual impunity.'

Raoul had at any rate the courage to stand in front of
Madame Fauvel, protecting her with his body and ready to
receive a bullet.

'Believe me, uncle . . .' he began.

A threatening gesture from the banker interrupted him.

'I have had enough,' he said, 'lies and infamy of that sort!
Cease your odious comedy, of which I am no longer the dupe.'

'I swear to you—'

'Spare yourself the trouble of denying anything. Can
you not see that I know everything? I know that my wife's
diamonds are in pawn. I know the author of the robbery for
which Prosper was arrested and put in prison!'

Madame Fauvel had fallen upon her knees. The moment
she had so long feared had come at last. She could see that
she was lost, and with suppliant gestures and a face bathed
in tears, she sobbed:

'Pardon, André, I beseech you, pardon!'

The sound of his wife's voice moved him to the bottom of
his soul. He recalled their twenty years of happiness, and at
that memory his heart was filled with sadness and the words
of forgiveness came to his lips.

'Wretched woman,' he murmured, 'wretched woman! What
have I done to you? Without a doubt I loved you too much, and
let you know too much. Everything in this world gets monoto-
nous, even happiness. How low you have fallen, Valentine! And
yet even if my love had ceased to please you, surely the thought
of your children ought to have preserved you?'

M. Fauvel spoke slowly and with an effort. Raoul, who
was following him closely, divined that though the banker
knew a great deal, he did not know all. He realized that he
was the victim of deceptive appearances. He thought there
was a possibility of an explanation.

'Sir . . .' he began, 'deign, I pray you—'

The sound of Raoul's voice was sufficient to break the
charm and reawaken the banker's anger.

'Ah, silence!' he cried with an oath. 'Silence!'

There was a long silence broken only by Madame Fauvel's sobs. At last the banker spoke:

'I came with the intention of surprising and killing you both. I have surprised you, but I cannot kill an unarmed man.'

Raoul tried to protest.

'Let me speak!' M. Fauvel interrupted. 'Your life is in my hands, is it not? The law excuses a wronged husband's anger, but I do not desire its shelter. I see a revolver like this upon your mantelpiece, take it and defend yourself.'

'Never!'

'Defend yourself!' the banker repeated, raising his arm. 'Defend yourself; if not—'

When Raoul saw M. Fauvel's revolver pointed at him, he was frightened and picked up his own weapon.

'Take your stand in one corner of the room,' the banker went on. 'I will take my place in the opposite one; at the first stroke of the clock, which will be in a few seconds, we will fire together.'

They took up their positions. But the scene was too terrible for Madame Fauvel to bear. She got up and stood between the two men facing her husband.

'Have pity, André,' she groaned, 'let me tell you the truth, do not kill him.'

This outburst of a mother's love M. Fauvel took to be the cry of the adulterous woman defending her lover. He seized his wife by the arm and threw her on one side. But she returned, and rushing to Raoul she put her arms round him, saying:

'Kill me, and me alone, for I am the guilty one!'

At these words a wave of blood mounted to the banker's head, he took aim at them and fired. Neither Raoul or Madame Fauvel falling, he fired again, three times in all, and he had raised his revolver for the fourth time when a man fell into the room, snatched the weapon from his hand, knocking him down as he did so, and rushed to Madame Fauvel.

It was M. Verduret whom Cavaillon had at last managed to find, but who did not know that Madame Gypsy had unloaded the banker's revolver.

'Thank God!' he cried. 'She is not touched.'

The banker was on his feet again.

'Leave me,' he said, struggling, 'I want my revenge.'

M. Verduret had him by the wrists, and was leaning forward to bring his face close to the banker's and give his words a greater force.

'Thank God,' he said to him, 'for sparing you from a horrible crime; the anonymous letter misled you.'

It never occurred to M. Fauvel to ask who this man was, or where he obtained his information.

'My wife admits that she is guilty!' he said.

'Yes, she is,' M. Verduret replied, 'but not of what you think. Do you know who this man is, whom you wish to kill?'

'Her lover.'

'No, but her son!'

This well informed unknown man's presence seemed to frighten Raoul more than M. Fauvel's threats. But he had presence of mind enough to say:

'That is true.'

The banker seemed to be going mad. His haggard eyes wandered from one to the other; but suddenly the idea struck him that they were playing with him.

'What you tell me is impossible!' he cried. 'Where are your proofs!'

'Proofs,' M. Verduret replied, 'you shall have; listen.'

Rapidly he sketched the main facts of the drama he had discovered. The truth was very terrible to M. Fauvel, but as he listened to the story he recognized the fact that he still loved his wife, and his heart suggested that he should pardon her remote fault, which had been expiated by a life of devotion. But his self-respect cried out for vengeance, though without Raoul he would not have hesitated to forgive her. But Raoul stopped him.

'Is that your son,' he asked his wife, 'the man who has robbed us?'

Madame Fauvel was too overwhelmed to speak. Fortunately M. Verduret was there.

'Oh,' he replied, 'your wife will tell you that this young man is indeed the son of Gaston de Clameran, she believes it, she is sure of it; but to more easily dispoil her they have shamelessly deceived her.'

Raoul, thinking no one would notice him, had skilfully manoeuvred towards the door. But M. Verduret had anticipated this movement and stopped him just as he was disappearing.

'Where are you going, my pretty boy?' he said, bringing him back into the middle of the room. 'Before separating, let us have a proper explanation.'

M. Verduret's jeering and satirical tones were like rays of light to Raoul. He recoiled in terror, murmuring 'The Clown!'

'Quite right,' the fat man replied, 'quite right. Have you any doubt about it?'

He turned up his coat sleeve, leaving his arm bare and went on.

'If you are not sure, examine this fresh wound. Don't you know the clumsy fellow who one fine night as I passed the Rue Bourdaloue rushed at me with an open knife in his hand? Ah! You don't deny it? That is so much gained. In that case perhaps you will be kind enough to tell us your little story.'

But Raoul was a prey to one of those terrors which contract the throat and prevent speech.

'You are silent,' M. Verduret went on; 'is it modesty? Modesty goes well with talent, and for your age you are a most accomplished scoundrel!'

M. Fauvel was listening without understanding. 'Into what an abyss of shame we are fallen!' he groaned.

'Make your mind easy, sir,' M. Verduret replied seriously. 'After what I have been obliged to let you know, there is not much more to tell. This is the rest of the story:

'On leaving Mihonne, after hearing the unfortunate story of Mademoiselle Valentine de la Verberie, Clameran went to London at once.

'He quickly found the farmer's wife to whom Gaston's son had been entrusted. But here a discovery awaited him. He learned that the child registered in the name of Raoul Valentin Wilson had died of croup when it was six months old.'

Raoul tried to protest.

'Someone has told you that,' he began.

'Yes, my boy, they have, and I have evidence to prove it.'

M. Verduret took from his pockets several documents with official stamps upon them.

'Here are,' he went on, 'the statements of the farmer's wife, her husband and four witnesses; here is a birth certificate and death certificate, properly authenticated by the French ambassador. Are you satisfied now, my pretty boy?'

'Then,' M. Verduret resumed, 'Clameran thought he could get money from Madame Fauvel without the child; he was mistaken. What was he to do? He is an ingenious rascal. Of all the scoundrels of his acquaintance he chose this one.'

Madame Fauvel was in a pitiable state, but she seemed to see a gleam of hope. Her long anxiety had been so horrible that the truth came as a welcome relief.

'Is it possible,' she stammered, 'is it possible?'

'What,' said the banker, 'can such crimes happen in our day?'

'All this is false!' Raoul audaciously affirmed. M. Verduret made his answer to Raoul only.

'The gentleman desires proof,' he said with ironical deference, 'he shall be obliged. I have just left a friend of mine, M. Pilot, who has come from London and is well informed. Tell me what you think of this little story he has just told me.'

'About 1847, Lord Murray, who is a great and generous nobleman, had a jockey named Spencer, of whom he was particularly fond. At Epsom the jockey had a fall and was killed.

'Lord Murray was very much upset, and having no children of his own he declared that he would adopt Spencer's son, who was then four years old.

'The nobleman kept his word. James Spencer was brought up like the heir to a large estate. He was a charming child, pretty and intelligent.

'Till he was sixteen James gave his protector every satisfaction. Unfortunately at that age he got into bad company and went wrong.

'Lord Murray, who was indulgence itself, forgave him many faults, but one fine day, finding out that his adopted son had been forging his signature, he turned him out.

'Now, for four years James Spencer had been living in London on his wits, when he met Clameran, who offered him 25,000 francs to play a part in a comedy.'

Raoul had no need to hear more.

'You are a detective?' he asked.

The fat man smiled.

'Just now I am only a friend of Prosper's. According as you act, I shall be one or the other.'

'What do you want?'

'Where are the 350,000 francs which were stolen?'

The young thief hesitated a moment.

'They are here,' he replied at last.

'Good! I knew it, and I know they are hidden in that cupboard. Give them to me!'

Raoul understood that the game was up. He took several packets of banknotes and an enormous packet of pawn-tickets from the cupboard and handed them over.

'Very well,' M. Verduret said as he looked through what Raoul had given him, 'very well, you have acted wisely.'

Raoul had reckoned upon this moment, when M. Verduret's attention was occupied, to make his escape. He gently approached the door, and opening it quickly, disappeared, locking it after him, for the key was outside.

'He is off!' cried M. Fauvel.

'Naturally,' M. Verduret replied, without turning his head, 'I thought he would be.'

'But—'

'What! Do you want this story known? Do you want to tell before the magistrate the story of the conspiracy of which your wife has been the victim?'

'Oh . . . sir!'

'Let the rascal go then. Here is the 350,000 francs and the tickets of the things pawned by him. Let us be satisfied. He has still got 50,000 francs, but so much the better. That sum will enable him to get out of the country and we shall hear no more of him.'

Like everyone else, M. Fauvel submitted to M. Verduret's will. The banker had just begun to realize that something dearer than his life had been preserved. His expressions of gratitude were not long in coming. He seized M. Verduret's hands almost as if he was going to raise them to his lips, and in a voice full of emotion, said:

'How can I ever prove to you the extent of my gratitude, sir? How can I repay you for the immense service you have rendered me?'

M. Verduret reflected.

'I have a favour to ask you, sir,' he began.

'You, a favour from me? Speak, sir! My person as well as my fortune is at your disposal.'

'Ah, well, sir, I will admit I am a friend of Prosper's. Will you help him to rehabilitate himself? You can do so much for him! He loves Mademoiselle Madeleine—'

'Madeleine shall be his wife, sir,' M. Fauvel interrupted; 'I swear it. I will reinstate him and with such éclat that no one will dare to reproach him with my fatal mistake.'

The fat man went to get his hat and cane from the corner of the room.

'You will excuse my importuning you,' he said, 'but Madame Fauvel—'

'André!' the poor woman murmured. 'André!'

The banker hesitated for a few seconds, and then bravely making up his mind, he ran to his wife and clasped her in his arms, saying:

'No, I will not be fool enough to struggle against my heart! I do not pardon, Valentine, I forget. I forget everything.'

M. Verduret's business at Vésinet was finished, so he went out without even wishing the banker good-bye, got into the carriage which had brought him, and set off to the *Hôtel du Louvre* as fast as possible. His mind was full of anxiety. Raoul was disposed of. Was it possible to hand over Clameran to justice without compromising Madame Fauvel?

'There is,' he thought, 'only one way. A suggestion of poisoning must come from Oloron. I can go there and work up public opinion, then there will be an inquiry. But all that requires time, and Clameran is too well warned not to escape.'

He was grieving at his impotence when the carriage stopped at the *Hôtel du Louvre*. It was nearly dark. There was a crowd of a hundred persons in the hotel porch, who seemed to be talking of some serious event.

'What has happened?' asked M. Verduret of one of the crowd.

'A very strange thing, sir,' the man replied; 'for I saw him clearly at the seventh attic-window. He was half-naked and they tried to seize him, but with the agility of a monkey or of a somnambulist he jumped on to the roof shouting out that he was being murdered.'

When the man looked round he was annoyed to find that his questioner had disappeared.

'It might be he,' M. Verduret thought, 'the fright may have turned his brain.'

With the help of his elbows M. Verduret had got inside and found Fanferlot with three other men waiting at the foot of the grand staircase.

'Ah, well!' M. Verduret cried.

The three men saluted simultaneously.

'The chief!' they said.

'Well, what is it?' the fat man said.

'I had no chance at all, sir,' Fanferlot said in a grieved tone, 'I had no chance at all.'

'Then it is Clameran who—?'

'Yes. When he saw me this morning he went off like a hare. When he got to the Boulevard des Écoles an idea suddenly occurred to him, and he came here. Very likely he came for his money. He went in; what did he see? My three comrades here. The sight was to him like a hammer blow on the forehead. He lost his reason.'

'But where is he?'

'At the Prefecture without doubt. I saw the policemen bind him and put him in a carriage.'

'Then come along.'

M. Verduret and Fanferlot found Clameran in one of the cells reserved for dangerous guests. They had put him in a strait-jacket and he was struggling fiercely while three men and a doctor were trying to make him swallow a draught.

'Help,' he was shouting, 'help! Don't you see him? It is my brother, he is coming towards me, he wants to poison me!'

M. Verduret took the doctor on one side to ask him a few questions.

'The poor wretch is doomed,' the doctor replied; 'this kind of derangement is incurable. He thinks people are trying to poison him, he will refuse food and drink, and whatever we do he will die of starvation, after suffering all the tortures of poison.'

M. Verduret shuddered as he went out.

'Madame Fauvel is saved,' he murmured, 'since God has punished Clameran.'

'But with all that,' Fanferlot grumbled, 'I get nothing for my pains.'

'Quite right,' M. Verduret replied, 'Dossier No.113 will not have to come out again. But before the end of the month I will give you a letter to take to one of my friends, and what you lose in glory you will gain in money.'

CHAPTER XXV

FOUR days later, M. Lecoq—the official Lecoq—was pacing up and down his private room and continually looking at the clock.

At last he rang his bell and Madame Nina and Prosper Bertomy were shown in.

'Ah!' said M. Lecoq. 'You are punctual, you lovers.'

'We are not lovers, sir,' Madame Gypsy replied, 'we received strict orders from M. Verduret to unite once more. He made an appointment with us here in your office.'

'Very well,' said the celebrated detective, 'wait a minute or two while I let him know you are here.'

For more than a quarter of an hour Nina and Prosper remained alone without exchanging a word. At last the door opened and M. Verduret appeared.

They wished to rush towards him, but he kept them in their places with an irresistible glance.

'You came here,' he said to them in a hard voice, 'to learn the secret of my conduct. I promised, and I will keep my word, however painful it is to me; listen to me—

'My best friend is a fine young fellow named Caldas. Eighteen months ago he was the happiest of men. Madly in love with a young woman, he imagined that she loved him.'

'Yes,' cried Gypsy, 'yes, she did love him!'

'Very well. She loved him so much that one fine day she went off with another man. At first Caldas, mad with grief, wanted to kill himself. Then on reflection he decided it would be better to live and have his revenge.'

'What then?' Prosper stammered.

'Then Caldas revenged himself in his own way, which means that he displayed his immense superiority over the other man in the sight of the woman who had deceived him.

Weak, cowardly and stupid the other man was in the depths
of misfortune; the powerful hand of Caldas rescued him. You
have understood, have you not? The woman is Nina; you are
the seducer; as for Caldas—'

With a violent gesture he pulled off his wig and whiskers,
and the clever, proud head of the real Lecoq appeared.

'Caldas!' Nina cried.

'No, not Caldas, nor Verduret any longer, but Lecoq the
detective!'

After a moment's silence for Prosper and Nina to recover
from their astonishment, M. Lecoq turned to Prosper and said:

'It is not to me alone that you owe your safety. A woman,
having the courage to trust in me, has rendered my task easy.
This woman is Mademoiselle Madeleine; to her I swore that
M. Fauvel should never know. Your letter made my plans
impossible.'

He tried to go back into his room, but Nina barred the way.

'Caldas,' she said, 'I implore you, I am so unhappy! Ah, if
you knew, forgive me . . . have pity on me!'

Prosper left M. Lecoq's room by himself.

The 15th of last month was celebrated, at the Church of Notre
Dame de Lorette, the marriage of M. Prosper Bertomy and
Mademoiselle Madeleine Fauvel.

The banking establishment is still in the Rue de Provence,
but M. Fauvel thinks of retiring, and the name of the firm
has been changed to *Prosper Bertomy & Co*.

THE END

THE DETECTIVE STORY CLUB

THE DETECTIVE STORY CLUB

FOR DETECTIVE CONNOISSEURS

recommends

AN ENTIRELY NEW

EDGAR WALLACE

The Terror

THE NOVEL OF THE MOST SUCCESSFUL DETECTIVE PLAY OF RECENT YEARS

EDGAR WALLACE, greatest of all detective writers, has given us, in *The Terror*, one of his most amazing thrillers, packed with dramatic incident and breathless suspense. A sensational success as a play, it has been made into as exciting a film, and now comes the book to provide hours of wonderful reading for all who enjoy a first-rate detective story in Edgar Wallace's characteristic style. Follow the unravelling of the mystery of the lonely house throughout whose dark corridors echoed the strange notes of an organ. Where did it come from and who played it? Whose was the hooded form which swept down in the night unseen upon its prey and dragged its victim to destruction? Follow the clues as suspicion moves from one inmate of that strange house to another. Experience a thrill on every page, until the biggest thrill of all comes with the solution of the mystery. *The Terror* proves, once again, that there are many imitators—but only *one* Edgar Wallace!

LOOK FOR THE MAN WITH THE GUN

THE DETECTIVE STORY CLUB

FOR DETECTIVE CONNOISSEURS

recommends

"The Man with the Gun."

MR. BALDWIN'S FAVOURITE

THE LEAVENWORTH CASE

By ANNA K. GREEN

THIS exciting detective story, published towards the end of last century, enjoyed an enormous success both in England and America. It seems to have been forgotten for nearly fifty years until Mr. Baldwin, speaking at a dinner of the American Society in London, remarked : " An American woman, a successor of Poe, Anna K. Green, gave us *The Leavenworth Case*, which I still think one of the best detective stories ever written." It is a remarkably clever story, a masterpiece of its kind, and in addition to an exciting murder mystery and the subsequent tracking down of the criminal, the writing and characterisation are excellent. *The Leavenworth Case* will not only grip the attention of the reader from beginning to end but will also be read again and again with increasing pleasure.

CALLED BACK

By HUGH CONWAY

BY the purest of accidents a man who is blind accidentally comes on the scene of a murder. He cannot see what is happening, but he can hear. He is seen by the assassin who, on discovering him to be blind, allows him to go without harming him. Soon afterwards he recovers his sight and falls in love with a mysterious woman who is in some way involved in the crime. . . . The mystery deepens, and only after a series of memorable thrills is the tangled skein unravelled.

LOOK FOR THE MAN WITH THE GUN

THE DETECTIVE STORY CLUB

FOR DETECTIVE CONNOISSEURS

recommends

"The Man with the Gun."

THE PERFECT CRIME

THE FILM STORY OF

ISRAEL ZANGWILL'S famous detective thriller, THE BIG BOW MYSTERY

A MAN is murdered for no apparent reason. He has no enemies, and there seemed to be no motive for any one murdering him. No clues remained, and the instrument with which the murder was committed could not be traced. The door of the room in which the body was discovered was locked and bolted on the inside, both windows were latched, and there was no trace of any intruder. The greatest detectives in the land were puzzled. Here indeed was the perfect crime, the work of a master mind. Can you solve the problem which baffled Scotland Yard for so long, until at last the missing link in the chain of evidence was revealed?

LOOK OUT
FOR FURTHER SELECTIONS FROM THE DETECTIVE STORY CLUB—READY SHORTLY

LOOK FOR THE MAN WITH THE GUN